*Emma didn't know
what her experience with men
in the past had been.*

Not much, apparently, because the doctor had told her she was still a virgin. Still, she suspected that Sheriff Tucker Malone was the sexiest man she'd ever laid eyes on. His brown hair was silver at the temples, but the strength and intensity in his dark eyes always awed her so much, her mouth went dry.

Ever since he'd taken her to the hospital, this... electricity crackled between them. Whenever she was close to him, she wanted to get closer. The golden sparks in his brown eyes now told her he might want that, too.

"Emma," he said, his voice husky.

She was afraid to move, afraid to answer him, afraid he'd back away. So she just looked up at him, wanting something she couldn't name, wanting to get to know him, wanting the man-woman connection she'd felt with him from the night they'd met....

* * * * *

Turn the page for the exciting conclusion of
Silhouette Romance's
STORKVILLE, USA series—

Dear Reader,

There's something for *everyone* in a Silhouette Romance, be it moms (or daughters!) or women who've found—or who still seek!—that special man in their lives. Just revel in this month's diverse offerings as we continue to celebrate Silhouette's 20th Anniversary.

It's last stop: STORKVILLE, USA, as Karen Rose Smith winds this adorable series to its dramatic conclusion. A virgin with amnesia finds shelter in the town sheriff's home, but will she find lasting love with *Her Honor-Bound Lawman*? *New York Times* bestselling author Kasey Michaels brings her delightful trilogy THE CHANDLERS REQUEST… to an end with the sparkling bachelor-auction story *Raffling Ryan*. *The Millionaire's Waitress Wife* becomes the latest of THE BRUBAKER BRIDES as Carolyn Zane's much-loved miniseries continues.

In the second installment of Donna Clayton's SINGLE DOCTOR DADS, *The Doctor's Medicine Woman* holds the key to his adoption of twin Native American boys—and to his guarded heart. *The Third Kiss* is a charmer from Leanna Wilson—a must-read pretend engagement story! And a one-night marriage that began with "The Wedding March" leads to *The Wedding Lullaby* in Melissa McClone's latest offering.…

Next month, return to Romance for more of THE BRUBAKER BRIDES and SINGLE DOCTOR DADS, as well as the newest title in Sandra Steffen's BACHELOR GULCH series!

Happy Reading!

Mary-Theresa Hussey

Mary-Theresa Hussey
Senior Editor

Please address questions and book requests to:
Silhouette Reader Service
U.S.: 3010 Walden Ave., P.O. Box 1325, Buffalo, NY 14269
Canadian: P.O. Box 609, Fort Erie, Ont. L2A 5X3

Her
Honor-Bound Lawman

KAREN ROSE SMITH

Nancy,
Have a happy
Thanksgiving.
All my best,
Karen Rose Smith

SILHOUETTE *Romance*

Published by Silhouette Books

America's Publisher of Contemporary Romance

Special thanks and acknowledgment are given to
Karen Rose Smith for her contribution to the
Storkville, USA, series.

To Jeanne Smith with thanks.

Author's note:
Guardianship/custody proceedings have been adapted
for purposes of the storyline.

 SILHOUETTE BOOKS

ISBN 0-373-19480-3

HER HONOR-BOUND LAWMAN

Visit Silhouette at www.eHarlequin.com

Printed in U.S.A.

Books by Karen Rose Smith

Silhouette Romance

*Adam's Vow #1075
*Always Daddy #1102
*Shane's Bride #1128
†Cowboy at the Wedding #1171
†Most Eligible Dad #1174
†A Groom and a Promise #1181
The Dad Who Saved
    Christmas #1267
‡Wealth, Power and a
    Proper Wife #1320
‡ Love, Honor and a
    Pregnant Bride #1326
‡Promises, Pumpkins and
    Prince Charming #1332
The Night Before Baby #1348
‡Wishes, Waltzes and a Storybook
    Wedding #1407
Just the Man She Needed #1434
Just the Husband She Chose #1455
Her Honor-Bound Lawman #1480

Silhouette Special Edition

Abigail and Mistletoe #930
The Sheriff's Proposal #1074

Silhouette Books

Fortunes of Texas
Marry in Haste...

*Darling Daddies
†The Best Men
‡ Do You Take This Stranger?

Previously published under the pseudonym Kari Sutherland

Silhouette Romance

Heartfire, Homefire #973

Silhouette Special Edition

Wish on the Moon #741

KAREN ROSE SMITH

lives in Pennsylvania with her husband of twenty-nine
years. She believes in happily-ever-afters and enjoys writing about them. A former teacher, she now writes romances
full-time. She likes to hear from readers, and they can write
to her at: P.O. Box 1545, Hanover, PA 17331.

STORKVILLE, USA

Storkville folks hardly remember the day
the town bore another name—because the
residents keep bearing bundles of joy! No
longer known for its safe neighborhoods and
idyllic landscape, Storkville is baby-bootie
capital of the world! We even have a legend
for the explosion of "uplets"—"When the
stork visits, he bestows many bouncing
bundles on those whose love is boundless!"
Of course, some—Gertie Anderson—still
insist a certain lemonade recipe, which
is "guaranteed" to help along prospective
mothers, is the real stork! But whether the
little darlings come from the cabbage patch
or the delivery room, Storkville folks never
underestimate the beauty of holding a
child—or the enchantment of first love
and the wonder of second chances....

Prologue

Sheriff Tucker Malone set down the sheaf of papers in his hand and pushed away from the desk in his office. Rising to his feet, he rolled his shoulders and went to stand at the window. He was too distracted to work, and the distraction was a woman named Emma.

Halloween night in Storkville, Nebraska, was usually quiet with only a few reports of pranks. He'd stayed late tonight in case he was needed. He'd stayed late tonight because he was unsettled by his reactions to a woman who couldn't remember her own name. Fortunately she'd been wearing a necklace with "Emma" engraved on it. But that's the only clue he'd had to begin his investigation.

Turning away from the window, he picked up the snapshot of her that lay on his desk. He'd taken it so he could fax it to surrounding towns. Certainly she belonged somewhere...to someone. A mugger had stolen her purse, as well as her overnight satchel, and with them anything that had identified her. No one in Storkville knew her. But she couldn't have come too far. There had been no abandoned vehicles around the town. It was a mystery.

Her sparkling green eyes stared up at him from the photograph, and her curly, dark coppery-red hair surrounded her face like a soft cloud. Her skin was so delicate, her smile so sweet, and whenever he looked at her a protective urge surged through him....

Get a grip, he scolded himself. *Find out who she is so you can send her back where she belongs.*

She'd spent the last three days under his roof, and it was driving him crazy. For the past two months Emma had been staying with Gertie Anderson who had witnessed her mugging and fall. But when Gertie's family had swept in from Sweden as an unexpected surprise, there hadn't been room for Emma. Before Tucker's better sense had caught his words, he'd offered her a room in his house.

Hoping Emma had turned in by now—it was almost eleven—he grabbed his leather bomber jacket from the old-fashioned clothes tree and snatched his Stetson from the rack on the wall. After he left his office, he stopped at an open doorway and bid Earl Grimes and Barry Sanchek a peaceful night.

The dispatcher, Cora Beth Harper, smiled at him as he passed her desk. "You've been putting in some long hours. Take care driving." Cora Beth had coal black hair that Tucker suspected was helped by a bottle of dye. She was plump with a voice that could stay calm in any situation, and she liked to mother everyone.

"Page me if you need me," he said as he usually did, and she nodded as he went out the door.

The Cedar County Sheriff's Department's black SUV sat at the curb. He pulled out the keys and pressed the remote to unlock it. As he climbed inside, he thought about the three years he'd lived in Storkville and the relative peace he'd found here. Taking a job as interim sheriff had probably saved his sanity as well as his career...although being sheriff in Storkville, Nebraska was a world away from being an undercover cop in Chicago. But the citizens of Storkville had liked the way he'd worked and elected him to a four-year term. This place, as well as his job, had given his life rhythm again and maybe even some meaning.

Streetlights illuminated residential areas as Tucker briefly cruised through them, making sure everything was quiet, everything was the way it should be, even though he realized that behind closed doors, sometimes nothing was the way it should be.

A short time later, he turned into the driveway to the garage attached to a two-story Colonial and pressed the remote for the double door. Now and then he still wondered why he'd bought a house this big. But it had been at a discount price because it needed fixing up. It had three bedrooms and a bath upstairs, a living room, large kitchen, and small den downstairs. And an unfinished basement.

It wasn't as if he had dreams of a family in the future. He'd given up those fantasies when he'd signed his divorce papers. Actually, he'd given up those fantasies the night—

Cutting off the memories he wouldn't tolerate, he pulled in beside his truck, lowered the garage door and climbed out of the SUV. When he opened the door leading down a short hall, he headed for the kitchen. The light was still burning over the sink. Emma must have left it on for him.

After he shrugged out of his jacket, he hung it on the

peg on the wall, his hat on the rack atop it. As he strode into the kitchen, he heard a low noise—the murmur of the TV.

Apparently Emma hadn't turned in yet.

The sound of Tucker's SUV pulling into the driveway had alerted Emma to his return. He'd said he would be late. She'd decided to wait up for him, to spend a few minutes with one of the few people she felt familiar with. The bump on her head from her fall had wiped out her past, and she was struggling to deal with that. What if she never remembered? What if she had to just go on from here?

Aunt Gertie, Tucker, and the workers at the day-care center where she volunteered were the only people she knew in the world. When Tucker had offered her a room under his roof, she'd been reluctant to accept, but Aunt Gertie—as most of the town called her—had soothed Emma's doubts with something she'd already known deep in her soul. Aunt Gertie had said, "Tucker Malone is the most honorable man I know. He'll keep you safe, and he'll do everything in his power to find out who you are."

Hearing the garage door close, Emma took a deep breath. She didn't know what her experience with men in the past had been. Not much, apparently, because after the doctor at the hospital had examined her, he'd told her she was still a virgin. Whatever it had been, she suspected Tucker Malone was the sexiest man she'd ever laid eyes on.

She heard his boots on the linoleum in the kitchen. She heard him walk through the dining room. When he appeared in the doorway to the living room, her heart skipped a beat.

He was at least six-two, with dark brown hair, enhanced by a bit of silver at the temples, that skimmed the collar of his tan sheriff's shirt. His shoulders were broad, and the dark brown stripe that went down the sides of his trousers emphasized his long legs. Her gaze met his. As always, the strength and intensity she found in his dark brown eyes awed her, so much so that her mouth went dry. She'd learned he was a man of few words most of the time. He'd checked on her often when she'd been at Aunt Gertie's. Although she'd been under *his* roof for three days, she still didn't know much about him.

His brows arched up now, and she knew it was an inquiry asking why she was still up.

She motioned to the two glasses she'd set on a tray on the dark pine coffee table and managed to find her voice. "I thought you might like some cider."

Leaning against the doorway, not making a move to come sit beside her on the tan-and-green plaid sofa, he asked, "Did many kids come to the door for tricks or treats?"

"I gave out all of the candy and popcorn balls. But I have a few cookies left." She gestured to the dish sitting between the glasses.

Tucker crossed to her slowly, and she saw his gaze linger on her hair, then pass down the emerald green sweater and slacks that she wore. Everything inside of her seemed to race, and she felt heat stain her cheeks. She fingered the necklace around her neck, the only proof of who she was.

"Did you make these?" he asked gruffly.

She nodded.

When he'd invited her to stay with him, she'd accepted under the terms that she would cook and clean house in exchange for board.

Tucker picked up one of the cookies and ate it. "I haven't tasted a peanut butter cookie in years. They're good, Emma."

"Thank you," she murmured, studying his expression, wondering if the faint lines around his eyes had come from happy or sad times. His face was rugged rather than handsome, his jaw strong, his beard shadow evident now, adding to his masculine appeal.

Tucker broke eye contact and took the remote control from her hand. His fingers brushed her palm, and the heat from their contact infused her whole body. When his arm brushed hers as he lowered the volume on the TV, Emma's heart pounded. As she glanced at Tucker, she saw he was gazing at her. Ever since the night she'd been mugged and he'd taken her to the hospital, this... electricity had crackled between them. Whenever she was close to him, she wanted to get closer. The golden sparks in his brown eyes now told her he might want that, too.

"Emma," he said, his voice husky.

She was afraid to move, afraid to answer him, afraid he'd back away. So she just looked up at him, wanting something she couldn't name, wanting to get to know him, wanting the man-woman connection she'd felt with him from the night they'd met.

When he bent his head slowly, she guessed he was waiting for her to lean away. But she wasn't going anywhere. His arm came around her as his lips brushed hers. The brushing became a meeting, the meeting became a hunger, the hunger became a kiss that made bells ring and the earth move. Emma didn't know if she'd ever been kissed before, or what to do next, but her lips parted and Tucker's tongue became masterful and possessive and demanding. She gave herself up to all of it, reveling in his need as well as hers, in something she imagined was desire but seemed like so much more.

Lost in Tucker Malone, Emma was excited by every new sensation until abruptly he pulled away.

In a terse voice, he said, "That was a mistake, Emma. It won't happen again."

It took her a few moments to realize the magic was gone and Tucker regretted what had happened. Still trembling, she didn't want him to notice. She didn't want him to see how he'd affected her. Because he was right. The kiss *had* been a mistake.

She couldn't get involved with anyone until she remembered who she was.

Chapter One

When the extension in Tucker's office rang midafternoon on November first, he picked up his phone. "Malone here."

"Tucker? It's Roy Compton over in Omaha."

Roy was a detective in the Omaha police department. He was the man Tucker had notified in August to discuss Emma's situation. Tucker's heart pounded faster. "Do you have something for me?"

"Possibly. There's a man here in Omaha who filed a report that his daughter's missing. Her name was Emma and your Emma fits the description. The file's been nonactive because the report came in about six months ago after the father and daughter had a terrific argument. The girl moved out all of her possessions while he was at work. He doesn't have a current picture of his daughter and the one you faxed me isn't exactly clear. He says the hair looks the same. He's real anxious to make this identification, Tucker. Do you think you could drive her down here this afternoon?"

Tucker knew all about missing someone, about having hope and losing it. He was sure Emma would be as anxious as this father to find out if she was his daughter or not.

Looking quickly over the papers and forms on his desk, he decided everything there could wait. "I'll go talk to Emma, then give you a call to let you know when we'll arrive." One way or another they were going to settle this today. Emma needed answers to the questions in her life. And after that kiss last night that had disconcerted him more thoroughly than a kiss ever had...

Tucker finally admitted to himself that he had his own reasons for wanting Emma to figure out her identity. Last night's kiss had been a monumental mistake. He'd given into an urge that he'd denied since long before his divorce. Actually the urge hadn't been that strong until he'd met Emma, and last night...he'd felt the full effects of not having a woman in his bed for the past few years.

And Emma?

The stars in her eyes right after the kiss had told him he'd better get her out of his house as soon as possible.

Grabbing his hat and jacket, he headed for the parking lot.

As she had most days for the past two months, Emma was volunteering at the new day-care center that had opened next door to Gertie. Shortly after Gertie had taken Emma in, Emma had gotten restless and needed something productive to do. She'd volunteered to help at BabyCare. Everyone she came in contact with at the center commented on how good she was with the children, but she'd especially taken to the abandoned twins Sammy and Steffie, who'd been left at BabyCare a few days before Emma had been mugged.

Five minutes later, Tucker parked along the curb in

front of BabyCare, climbed out, and ducked his head against the cold wind as he approached the wraparound porch. Hannah Caldwell owned BabyCare, a sprawling three-story Victorian house that had answered a very necessary need in Storkville for working parents who wanted a safe haven where their children could be cared for.

After he opened the heavy wood door, he peered into the room on his right. There were playpens and playmats and women caring for children as young as six months and as old as five years. Emma was sitting on the floor on a quilt with Hannah. They were stacking blocks with Sammy and Steffie who were about a year old. Tucker usually kept his distance from children, and Sammy and Steffie with their reddish-brown hair and big blue eyes were no exception.

Standing at a changing table folding towels, Gertie Anderson saw Tucker and came toward him with a grin. She was in her late sixties with silver hair and brown eyes. Petite enough to flitter here and there, she had more energy than most people younger than she was. Since she lived next door to BabyCare, she helped out often when she wasn't riding around town in her motorized shopping cart. She'd been the first person to officially welcome Tucker to Storkville and had bought him a cup of coffee while she'd filled him in on the town and lots of its inhabitants. It hadn't taken Tucker long at all to see she had a heart of gold.

Coming over and stopping in front of him, her white-and-black oxford shoes almost touched his boots. "Is this an official visit or a friendly one?"

"Official *and* friendly," he replied. "I didn't think I'd find you here with all that company of yours in town. Are they still staying until Christmas?"

Gertie eyed him and he knew he should have tried to

make his question more subtle. "Is Emma getting in your way?"

In his way. That was an understatement. "I'm just afraid the gossips might start a few rumors."

"That didn't seem to be a consideration when you asked her to stay with you. Besides, everyone in this town knows you're as upright as the Statue of Liberty. They also know Emma has no place to go and no one to turn to." Gertie patted his arm. "You let me take care of the gossips. It's been so long since my family and I were all under the same roof together, they might stay forever! My sisters and nieces and nephews talk long into the night. I'm having a good time, Tucker. Maybe you should stop worrying about Emma being under your roof and just enjoy having her there."

"She might not be there much longer. I've gotten a lead."

"What kind of lead?"

"I can't say anything more till I talk with Emma. We have to drive to Omaha. Do you have enough help here that she can get away?"

"Sure we do. Penny Sue will be here shortly after school. Gwen's here, too. She's with the kids who are napping." Penny Sue Lipton was a fifteen-year-old who helped out at the day-care center after school. Gwenyth Parker Crowe, who was Hannah's cousin, was a relative newcomer to Storkville. She had married Ben Crowe a few weeks ago.

Emma's laughter floated across the large room, and Tucker's gaze went to her again. She was such a lovely woman, but so young, so vulnerable. Hannah, with her light brown hair, blocked Tucker's line of vision for a moment as she stooped to pick up Sammy who had scrambled away from the quilt. When she caught him, he let out a squeal and wriggled away, heading toward Emma where Steffie was already sitting contentedly in her lap.

"I have a feeling about Emma and those twins," Gertie said.

Tucker glanced at her. "What kind of feeling?"

She nodded toward them. "Hannah might have temporary custody, and she might be good with the babies, but you watch Sammy and Steffie with Emma. They act as if they've known her all their lives. I know she can't be their mother, but there's got to be some kind of connection."

"I don't know, Aunt Gertie. If this lead pans out, I don't see how there *can* be a connection. Maybe we'll have some answers by the end of the day."

Tucker strode across the large room past giant balls and colorful toys, then past the low table where one of Hannah's assistants sat with a group of children. He tried not to hear their chatter or laughter. Children reminded him of Chad, and memories of Chad reminded him he'd made mistakes in his life that were unforgivable.

Emma rose to her feet when she saw Tucker, holding Steffie in her arms. She was wearing a long red corduroy jumper with a white pullover underneath. Part of her curly hair was tied up in a ponytail while the rest hung silky, loose and free. He remembered the scent of her shampoo when he'd kissed her. He remembered the softness of her lips, the faint freckles on the bridge of her nose, her erotic sweetness....

Cutting off thoughts that had taken over his dreams and distracted him too many times to count today, he stopped with his boots at the edge of the quilt and nodded to Hannah. "I need to borrow Emma this afternoon. Aunt Gertie says you have enough help to manage."

"Sure do. Full staff today."

Steffie was looking up at Tucker curiously as if fascinated by his face or maybe his hat. She reached out her little arms to him and he took a step back.

"Tucker?" Emma asked him, studying him closely.

The little girl's big blue eyes beseeched him to hold her. He couldn't resist...and held his arms out, lifting her into them. She fingered the star on his shirt and then touched his cheek and smiled up at him like a little angel who'd dropped down from heaven. His heart ached and his chest tightened. The feel of her in his arms brought back so many memories—Chad laughing and squealing as Tucker tossed him up into the air, as he pushed him on the swing, as he read him a story at night. The pain of letting the memory surface was more than Tucker could take.

He handed Steffie back to Emma. "I got a call from a detective in Omaha. There's a man there who's looking for his daughter. Her name is Emma. The photo I faxed them didn't come through clearly and he'd like to see you...meet you and determine if you're his daughter."

Emma's face paled. "You want to leave now?"

"Yes. I'll call him and tell him we're on our way. Roy said the man was free anytime. I'll meet you outside."

Steffie's arms tangled around Emma's neck and the year-old laid her head on Emma's shoulder. Emma smoothed the baby's hair and lightly kissed her forehead. When she looked up, Tucker was already through the foyer and opening the outside door.

The sheriff was such an enigma to her. His reaction to Steffie just now... There'd been such pain in his eyes and then such longing before he'd guarded himself, before he'd put Steffie back in Emma's arms.

Hannah had set Sammy in the playpen and a string of

red, yellow and blue beads kept his attention for the moment. Hannah held her arms out to Steffie, and Steffie went reluctantly to the woman who'd been her primary caretaker for the past two months. "Good luck," Hannah said to Emma.

"Thanks. I'm almost afraid to hope. I can come in tomorrow and help until my doctor's appointment at three-thirty."

"Are you feeling all right?"

"Fine. It's just a checkup. The neurologist wants to keep tabs on the headaches."

"Have you had any lately?" Hannah asked, concerned.

"Not since that last flashback...if you could call it that." She'd been here playing with Steffie and Sammy. All of a sudden, she'd had the vague memory of hanging baby clothes on a washline. Then she'd gotten a pounding headache. None of it made sense. If she was a virgin, she certainly didn't have any children of her own. Maybe she'd worked for someone who'd had children.

"I'll see you in the morning," she said to Hannah as she brushed her hand tenderly once more over Steffie's hair, then Sammy's.

After Emma said goodbye to Aunt Gertie, she took her coat from the hall closet and went outside on the porch. Tucker was standing there waiting for her.

A few minutes later, he'd driven down Main Street past businesses and houses and finally fields when Emma asked, "What happened in there, Tucker?"

There was a pause. "I don't know what you mean."

"With Steffie. I noticed before when you came into the day-care center, you stayed away from the children."

"You're imagining things," he said gruffly.

"I may have lost my memory, Tucker, but my eyesight is good. Don't you like children?"

"Children are fine. I'm just not a...family man, that's all."

"Where is your family?" she probed, wanting to know more about him, wanting to know why he was so quiet sometimes, wanting to know why he was so strong.

"I don't have any family."

"Your parents are...gone?" she asked hesitantly.

He glanced at her and was silent for a few moments, but eventually answered, "My mother left my father and me when I was a kid. She didn't like being married to a cop, and she wanted a different life than the one we had. She sent a few postcards and then we stopped hearing from her altogether."

"And your dad?"

After a moment, he responded, "My dad died in the line of duty when I was at the police academy. I searched for my mother after that, found out she'd been in an automobile accident about three years before and didn't make it."

"I'm sorry, Tucker."

He shrugged. "Life goes on."

That sounded a little too glib to her and didn't explain how he'd reacted to the children. But she could see he didn't want to talk about it. He'd been so kind to her, so protective since that night when he'd taken her to the hospital, that she didn't want to pry where she shouldn't. "Aunt Gertie told me you've lived in Storkville about three years. Where did you live before that?"

With a frown, he cast a quick glance at her. "Why all the questions, Emma?"

She fiddled with her seat belt. "I need something to

concentrate on. I can't just sit here wondering what's going to happen when we get to Omaha.''

He blew out a breath. "I see. I should have figured that out. I thought you might be asking because— Never mind, it doesn't matter. Before I moved to Storkville, I lived in Chicago.''

"You were a member of the police force there?''

"Oh yeah.''

"So why'd you come to Storkville?''

His jaw tensed for a moment, then he replied, "I needed a change, and Storkville certainly was that. You've heard how it got its name, haven't you?''

"No, I haven't.''

"I don't know how Gertie missed telling you that. Thirty-two years ago, a storm knocked out all the electricity in the town and there was a blackout that lasted quite a few days. Nine months later, a lot of babies were born. When the media in the surrounding areas heard about it, they dubbed the town Storkville. On the second year anniversary of the blackout, the town council officially renamed the town Storkville. Apparently there's always been a lot of multiple births here. And Aunt Gertie gave the town its motto—When The Stork Visits Storkville, He Bestows Many Bouncing Bundles On Those Whose Love Is Boundless.''

"You sound as if you don't believe that.''

"Some days I'm not sure what I believe.''

What had he seen, what had happened to persuade him to give up a life in Chicago and move here? But she knew he might not answer *that* question. So she asked another. "What made you become a police officer? Your dad?''

"I suppose. I said some days I don't know what I believe, but that's not quite true. My father taught me a code—a code of values, a code of behavior. He taught me right from wrong, and I saw him put it into practice. I never wanted to be anything else.''

"You're a lucky man, Tucker.''

He gave her more than a glance this time. "Why?''

Their gazes held for a moment, then he looked back at the road. But she could tell he was intensely interested in her answer. "You had a good man for a father who taught you the basis of being an adult. It sounds as if you've always known who you are. You're really blessed.''

The nerve in his jaw worked, and she had a feeling there was so much he hadn't told her, so much he wouldn't tell her. She went on, "Every minute of every day, I wonder who I am. I wonder what kind of parents I had. I wonder what they taught me and where I grew up and why I can't remember any of it. The neurologist said traumatic amnesia is selective in a way. I'm not sure I understand what he means, but have I selected not to remember my parents, not to remember my upbringing?''

"Your amnesia could very well have a physical cause, too, and in about another half hour, you might know a whole lot more. How about some music? Will that distract you?''

She'd rather keep talking to him. She'd rather keep learning about what he thought and what he felt and why he considered their kiss a great big mistake. But she suspected he wouldn't tell her that. She suspected he wouldn't tell her a lot of things.

If Emma had ever been to Omaha, she couldn't tell. None of it seemed familiar. Tucker knew exactly where he was going. When he parked near the police station, Emma took a deep breath.

He came around to her side of the truck and opened

the door for her. His dark brown eyes stared down at her steadily. "Are you ready?"

She nodded and took the large hand he gave her to help her step down from the truck. His palm had calluses, and the heat from his fingers seemed to warm her down deep inside. She was glad he was here with her. She was glad she didn't have to do this alone.

Tucker ushered her inside the six-story building where they were directed to Roy Compton's office. A tall, broad-shouldered man opened the door, shook Tucker's hand then hers, and introduced himself as Roy Compton. As soon as Emma stepped into his office, she was aware of another man also wearing a suit who had auburn hair, green eyes and looked to be in his fifties. She felt no flicker of recognition and her stomach somersaulted.

"Sheriff Malone, Emma, this is Robert Franz."

It didn't take long for a terribly disappointed look to come over the man's face, then he shook his head. "She's not my daughter. She's not my Emma."

Emma's breath caught, her heart pounded. He didn't know her. She might never find out who she was. But as soon as those thoughts clicked through her mind, she realized how distressed the man was, how agonizing this was for him. Without thinking twice, she crossed to him. "I'm sorry I'm not your daughter, Mr. Franz. I hope you find her. I hope you find her very soon."

Robert Franz's eyes grew moist. "I might never find her if she has anything to say about it. She thinks I want to run her life and she's probably right."

"But you're her father and as the days go by, she'll want that connection back. I know she will."

Franz studied Emma and then nodded as if her words had given him some hope.

* * *

Although Tucker had been unsettled by Emma's questions on the drive to Omaha, he realized her silence was just as disconcerting now. She wasn't a silent woman and her quietness worried him. Even in the midst of her own situation, her own confusion, she'd reached out to a man she didn't know to help him feel better. She was a special woman, a very young woman, probably in her early twenties. At thirty-seven, he felt a lifetime older than she was.

Emma's silence lasted until they returned to Tucker's house. He pulled into the garage next to his blue pickup truck. He should take it out for a run soon. He hadn't started it in two days. But he wasn't as concerned about his truck as he was about Emma. She'd stared into space on the drive home or out the window and he wished he could read the thoughts clicking through her head.

She climbed out of the SUV before he'd put the garage door down and started into the house. After he followed her, he found she'd thrown her coat over a stool at the counter and was washing her hands at the sink. "I'm going to make a meat loaf for supper and rice and green beans. I can whip up a batch of brownies for dessert if you'd like. It won't take too long."

Quickly she dried her hands, then moved to the refrigerator, taking out the ground beef. Her movements were almost frenetic, much too fast. She was hurrying and there was no reason to hurry.

"If you don't feel like cooking," he said, "I can go get some take-out. Do you like Chinese?"

"That won't be necessary. I'll have supper ready in an hour. Oh…maybe the meat loaf won't be done by then. Would you like barbecued beef instead?"

As she talked and moved, Tucker knew he had to put a stop to it. Crossing the room, he blocked her path as she tried to make a return trip to the refrigerator. "Talk to me, Emma."

"There's nothing to talk about."

"You're upset."

"Of course I'm upset, and that's why I need to do something."

She tried to go around him, but he caught her by the shoulders. "Stop."

"Tucker, don't," she protested, her voice quivering. "I don't want to think about what happened."

"It could happen again. I might get another lead we have to chase down."

Shaking her head, she tried to break free of his grasp. But he held her steady and, as he did, he saw tears come to her eyes.

"It's okay, Emma. It's okay to be disappointed and upset. I haven't seen you cry since this whole thing happened. If anyone deserves to cry, you do."

More tears welled in her eyes and spilled over, and he couldn't help but fold his arms around her and hold her close.

She held on to him.

He let his cheek rest against her hair. Everything about her was so feminine…so tempting…so vulnerable. What had been a comforting embrace became more for Tucker. Her hair against his jaw was as arousing as her soft breasts pressed against his chest. The desire that rolled through him whenever he saw her, let alone whenever he touched her, became a rush of heat throughout his body, inflaming his hunger for her. But she needed him right now and no woman had needed him in just this way for a very long time.

"We'll find out who you are. I've sent more inquiries to South Dakota and Wyoming, and I'll do it across the country if I have to." He rubbed his hand up and down her back. "And maybe you'll have more flashbacks. You're seeing the doctor tomorrow, aren't you?"

She leaned away from him slightly and nodded. "It was just looking into Mr. Franz's eyes that upset me. I wondered if anybody missed me that badly. But certainly they would have come looking for me if they had."

"I'm sure someone misses you, Emma. A great deal." Her upturned chin, her sparkling green eyes, the innocence he saw every time he looked at her, convinced him someone had to miss her tremendously.

"Thank you for being with me today, Tucker. Sometimes I feel as if I can handle anything—who I am, what I did, where I lived. I believe I'll find out any hour, any day. But then others— It was good to have you there."

"I don't need your thanks. I was doing my job." But as he said it, he knew that wasn't entirely true. Emma had become more than his job, and that was the problem.

"Do you become this personally involved with all the people you help?" she asked.

His answer would be a catch-22. He'd be in trouble either way. "I do what I have to do."

"But what do you *want* to do, Tucker?"

It was as if she knew everything in him was screaming at him to kiss her, to hold her in his arms more intimately, to give them both pleasure. But just because he'd given in to that impulse once, didn't mean he was going to give in again. His father had taught him discipline, and he'd honed it on his own over the years. It was a necessary trait in law enforcement. It was a necessary trait when a man held a vulnerable woman in his arms.

"I want to find out who you are, and I want to return you to wherever you belong," he answered her.

The startled look in her eyes became a hurt one. Pulling free of his arms, she straightened her shoulders. "I'm fine now. As you said, I have to get used to this type of thing happening...and I will. I'm not going to give up on finding out who I am anymore than you are. Maybe that's the problem. I haven't tried hard enough. I'll talk to the doctor about it tomorrow. Maybe I should even go door to door throughout Storkville, asking anyone and everyone if they've ever seen me. I had to be here for some reason. Someone should know me."

That's exactly what Tucker thought. But Emma's story had been in the Storkville paper and no one had come forward. Apparently no one was missing this beautiful young woman.

And Tucker wondered why.

The next morning Tucker was gone when Emma went down to the kitchen. She was relieved in a way, yet disappointed, too. Last night when he'd held her, she'd felt so secure, so safe. Being in his arms felt so right. But obviously he didn't feel the same way. She'd thought he was going to kiss her again. Apparently he was just giving her comfort, just doing part of his job. Yet she couldn't believe that the golden sparks in his dark brown eyes had been simply duty.

In the few days she'd been with him here in his house, she'd learned he was a complicated man. He'd worked in his den last night until supper. Then after supper, during which she hadn't said much at all, he'd gone back to his office at the sheriff's department. She'd gone to bed around ten and heard him come in shortly after. His room was next door to hers, and she could hear the clang of his belt as he undressed, his boots falling onto the floor. She could even hear the creak of his bed as he got in.

She didn't know who she was, yet she was having

these thoughts about a man she barely knew. She shook her head. Maybe the two went together. Maybe her thoughts were swirling around Tucker because he was the only stable person in her world right now.

After she nibbled on a piece of toast and drank a cup of tea, she walked the four blocks to the day-care center. When she'd first moved in, Tucker had wanted to drive her there in the mornings. But she liked walking in the crisp, cool air. She liked the quiet. She liked passing the people in the houses on the street. Every time she took the walk, she hoped something would trigger her memory.

As always, when Emma arrived at the day-care center, it bustled with activity as parents dropped off their children for the day. Emma helped them with their coats and then took them to play stations or the breakfast corner. Every chance she got, she played with Sammy and Steffie. Sometimes when she held them...she felt on the verge of remembering. But then afterwards she told herself she was being silly. She must just love babies.

The morning sped by and soon it was time to serve lunch. Emma worked beside Hannah and two other volunteers. "Gwen called this morning to let me know that she wouldn't be in," Hannah told her as she poured juice.

"How's she feeling?" Gwen had come to Storkville, trying to escape the effects of a difficult divorce. She'd been pregnant and just wanted some peace and quiet. Instead she'd fallen in love with Ben Crowe and married him.

"Her doctor told her she could deliver anytime, so she's sticking close to Ben and he's sticking close to her. He probably won't let her out of his sight for very long."

Emma laughed. "Is he the protective type?"

"Very. Even more so than Jackson, and Jackson and I have go-rounds about it now and then."

Hannah herself had just married in September to Jackson Caldwell. He was a pediatrician and the son of Jackson Caldwell Sr., who had been one of the wealthiest men in Storkville. Jackson had returned to the town when his father died six months ago. He and Hannah had the type of marriage that Emma admired. Anyone a mile away could see how much in love they were.

As soon as Hannah finished pouring juice, she and Emma served the children lunch. As usual there were spills and giggles, faces to be wiped, and energy to direct. It was almost three when Emma glanced at her watch and checked in with Hannah again.

"I'm going to spend a few minutes with Sammy and Steffie and then I'll have to leave."

"That's fine. Penny Sue will be coming in. You know, it's okay if you take a day off now and then. You don't have to come in every day."

"Nothing else seems quite as worthwhile as coming here and helping you."

Fifteen minutes later, Emma was sitting on the floor, holding Steffie and watching Sammy awkwardly push a walking toy in the shape of a train engine. He wasn't taking steps on his own yet, but it wouldn't be long. He'd just fallen and was deciding whether to cry or laugh when Tucker suddenly towered above them.

"I came to take you to your doctor's appointment."

"I can walk, Tucker. It's only a few blocks. You didn't have to interrupt your work."

"You're part of my work," he said briskly.

She wished that weren't so. She wished he'd come to drive her simply because he wanted to. "We have a few minutes before my appointment. There's coffee in the kitchen if you want some. I'll get the twins busy with something in the playpen and then we can go.''

Tucker looked down at the floor at Sammy and then at Steffie in Emma's arms. ''Right. A cup of coffee would be good. Come get me when you're ready to leave.''

As Emma watched him walk away, she again wondered what made him so uncomfortable being in the midst of children. She vowed to herself she'd find out what it was.

Soon.

Chapter Two

On the way to the doctor's office, Emma noticed Tucker was driving his truck rather than the sheriff's vehicle. "Do you have any leads on the twins?"

He shook his head. "They seem to have dropped out of midair the same way you did. I thought finding the monogram on that rattle left with them was a real clue."

Everyone but Tucker had missed the faint monogram on the sterling silver rattle that had been tucked in with the babies. It had led him to the McCormack estate and Quentin McCormack. But a DNA test had proved Quentin wasn't the father.

"What happens now?" Emma asked.

"I have one more lead. Someone I haven't interviewed yet. He's the butler on the McCormack estate who hires additional help for parties and the like. He's been away the past month or so on a family emergency, but he's expected back soon. I'm hoping he might have seen or heard something, or has some clue as to why that rattle was with the babies."

"Hannah's talking about adopting them," Emma said wistfully. "I'd love to consider it myself, but I can't. Not until I know who I am."

"I'm working on it, Emma," Tucker said, his mouth forming a straight, terse line.

She reached over and touched his arm. "I know you are. I know you're doing all you can."

Some of the tension went out of his shoulders. "You should be hopping mad I haven't found a clue about you."

"I know you work hard at your job, Tucker. I just have to trust that something will turn up when it's supposed to. Maybe I'll get my memory back on my own. I'm going to talk to the doctor today about working harder on that."

"He told you before not to push."

"Yes, he did. But he didn't say why. I need to feel I'm doing something positive to get my life back."

When Tucker pulled up in front of the office complex where several doctors were housed, he didn't let Emma off at the curb but climbed out and came around.

"Don't you have to get back to the office?" she asked.

"I've been putting in a lot of late hours. My time is my own this afternoon. Unless they page me."

"I don't want you to waste your time waiting. I can find my way home...I mean to your house." Tucker's house was starting to feel like a home and she knew that was dangerous.

"You let me worry about my time. I'll catch up on the latest issue of *People* magazine." A small smile played across his lips.

She laughed. Once in a while she saw a lighter side of Tucker, a side that might have been prevalent at one time. *Something else to explore,* she thought as they walked up the sidewalk, side by side, her elbow gently brushing his. Even that faint contact was enough to make her totally aware of him, totally aware of herself as a woman.

Inside the doctor's reception area, Tucker helped Emma with her royal blue coat, hanging it on a rack. It had been a present from Dana McCormack, Quentin's wife, when the weather turned colder. Only the clothes she'd worn the night of the mugging were hers. Hannah and Dana, almost the same size as she was, had given her spare garments that were seeing her through. But she wished she could get a job and start earning money again. She loved volunteering at the day-care center, but she didn't like depending on anyone else for the roof over her head and the food on her plate.

Tucker placed his hat on the rack above the coats and ran his hand through his hair. It was such thick, vibrant hair and she'd love to run *her* fingers through it. She'd love to...

Cutting off the thought, she headed for the reception-ist's window and checked in. Tucker had taken a seat, picked up a magazine and unzipped his jacket but hadn't shed it.

She'd no sooner taken the chair beside him when the door opened from the inner offices and the nurse called her name. She followed the white-uniformed woman to an examining room where the brunette took her blood pressure and pulse and told her the doctor would be in in a few minutes.

When Dr. Weisensale came in, he gave her a broad smile. "How are you today?"

A fatherly gentleman with white hair and a gray-white beard, he had always been kind to her. "I'm frustrated. I need to get my memory back so I can get on with my life. Can we try hypnosis?"

Dr. Weisensale studied her pensively. "Have you had anymore flashbacks?"

She'd called him about the shadowy remembrance of hanging baby clothes on a washline, how it had seemed like a memory, but yet unreal, too. Maybe something out of her imagination instead. "No, not since I phoned you."

"Do you ever feel as if you might remember? As if your last name and where you're from are teetering right on the edge of your consciousness?"

"Sometimes. Especially when I'm with the twins at the day-care center. That's what's so confusing. I know I can't be a mother, but maybe I was a nanny. Maybe I watched over children in my job. Everything about taking care of them comes so naturally."

Again he studied her. "Emma, I want you to think about something. Sometimes amnesia has a physical cause and sometimes it doesn't."

"You've mentioned that before."

"Your tests all came back clean and I want you to consider something. Sometimes amnesia around a trauma is self-induced. It's a possibility that you had a life you don't want to remember."

Emma's dismay must have shown on her face.

"I'm not saying that's the actuality," he went on, "but it's something to think about."

"I *do* want to remember, doctor."

His expression was kind. "You think you do, but your subconscious might think otherwise. Still, the fact that you're having any flashbacks is positive. I'd rather you waited to try hypnosis at least another month or two. I know how frustrating this must be, but you must be patient. It truly is better if you remember on your own."

"But what if I never remember? I need to have a life,

and I can't have a life without a Social Security number!" When she said it, she realized how preposterous that sounded. But in a way it was true. She couldn't work without one. She didn't even know if she could take a driving test without one.

"I'm sure you fall under some kind of special circumstances and that can be remedied if the amnesia lasts."

"I don't want to owe other people, doctor. First Aunt Gertie took me in, now Tucker. It's embarrassing sometimes."

"Something tells me, Emma, that you were a very independent woman, whoever you were before this bump on the head. I'll tell you what. Give it one more month. If you don't have any significant flashbacks, if nothing has changed, I'll contact a psychologist I know who's trained in hypnotherapy. Fair enough?"

Another month under Tucker's roof...unless she remembered on her own, unless he found another lead to her identity. But there was really nothing else she could do right now. "All right, another month. But then I see a hypnotherapist."

When Emma appeared in the waiting room, Tucker saw she was frowning, and after she went to the receptionist's window and spoke with her, she looked upset. But there was a couple sitting in the waiting room now and he wanted to talk to her in private. She took her coat from the rack with a determined yank and didn't wait for Tucker to help her with it. Then she was out the door and down the walk toward the truck before he zipped his jacket.

He caught up with her before she opened her door. "Emma, what's wrong?"

"Wrong? Nothing's wrong. Everything's just hunky-dory. I don't know who I am. I don't know where I should live. I don't even know my birth date. And on top of all that, Dr. Weisensale suggested again that maybe I don't *want* to remember any of that. If I don't want to remember my past, doesn't that make you wonder what kind of past I have?''

"I'm sure your past is very respectable." Tucker tried to be soothing.

"Respectable? I don't feel as if my *present* is respectable. Aunt Gertie took me in. Now you've taken me in. And Dr. Weisensale told his receptionist there was no charge for today. He thinks I'm a charity case. I'm not, Tucker. I want to get a job. I want to work. I want to—'' She bit her lower lip, and he could see her chin quiver.

Clasping her by the shoulders, he gazed into her beautiful green eyes that were shiny with tears. "I know this is frustrating for you. I wish I could do more to help."

"I don't want you to do more to help. I want to help myself. I asked about hypnotism, but Dr. Weisensale wants me to give it another month. A month, Tucker."

"Is staying with me so bad?" he teased, thinking about her spending another month under his roof...in the bedroom beside his.

She let out a breath with a sigh and then gave him a weak smile. "No, of course not."

He wanted to pull her into his arms and protect her. He wanted to set his lips on hers and taste her again. But instead, he lifted her chin with his thumb. "I think you need some perspective, time out of the house to enjoy yourself. Why don't we go to the diner for a quick supper, then catch a movie?"

"A movie?"

"Yeah. I can't remember the last time I went to a movie theater. And I know you can't, either," he said with a grin.

She looked startled for a moment, and then she laughed. "You're right about that. All right, Sheriff Malone, you're on. The blue-plate special and a movie. That should give me exactly the perspective I need."

Her eyes were sparkling now, and her lips turned up in the sweetest smile he'd ever seen. Quickly he released her, then opened the door for her. When she climbed inside, he shut it, wondering what in the hell he'd just gotten himself into.

As usual, Vern's Diner was bustling with a full capacity crowd. Tucker and Emma stood inside for a moment, searching for an empty table or booth. From a few feet away, Tucker felt glances on them.

A woman leaned over to the man who was with her and asked him, "Isn't that the woman who doesn't know who she is?"

Tucker could tell that Emma had overheard the comment, too. A shadow passed over her face, and he moved closer to her. "Maybe we should go to Chez Stork up the street. It would be quieter."

Chez Stork wasn't only quieter, but a lot more expensive and very elite. There was an aura of intimacy there that Tucker would rather avoid. But he didn't want Emma to feel uncomfortable.

Emma gazed up at him, her green eyes serious. "Would you rather leave? Just because I'm the talk of the town doesn't mean *you* should be."

"Talk doesn't bother me."

Emma nodded to a booth that had just been vacated. "Then let's get that table before somebody else does."

Tucker had never met a woman quite like Emma. She was feminine in every sense of the word and yet there was a strength in her that he had to admire. She was so different from Denise. But he put that thought out of his head as they walked toward the booth.

Almost there, Tucker spotted Ben Crowe, his wife Gwen and the nine-year-old boy they were going to adopt, Nathan.

Emma stopped and smiled at Gwen. "Hi, there. How are you feeling?"

"Very big. But I guess that's to be expected at this stage," the pretty blonde said with a laugh.

Ben addressed Emma and Tucker. "Coming out to eat was the only way I could get her to stop unpacking boxes."

Ben and Gwen had lived in her cottage since their wedding two weeks ago and now were moving into Ben's ranch house. Ever since Nathan had gotten into some trouble with older boys last month, Tucker and Ben had become more friendly.

"Do you need any help moving?" Tucker asked.

Ben shook his head. "Thanks for asking, but we finished up today. Now if I can just convince my wife that she has to take it easy until she has this baby…"

"I'm going to have a brother or sister," Nathan proudly informed them. "Ben's going to adopt both of us."

Ben ruffled Nathan's hair. "I sure am. And we'd better get going if you want to put the finishing touches on that science project."

Tucker tipped his hat to them. "Take care. And Gwen, if you need a proper escort to the hospital, just give a yell."

"I'll keep that in mind," she said with a grin.

After Tucker and Emma settled into the booth, Emma leaned toward him and whispered, "We're giving a shower for Gwen at the day-care center on Monday evening.''

"I'm sure she'll appreciate that.''

Leaning back again, she said, ''It was nice of you to offer to help them move.''

Tucker shrugged and picked up the menu, but he could feel Emma's eyes on him. ''What?'' he asked when he looked up and she didn't avert her gaze.

''What do you do for fun?'' she asked.

''In my spare time I work on the house—outside work in the summer, inside in the winter. I'm going to drywall the basement, maybe get some exercise equipment.''

''I didn't ask how you fill your spare time. What do you do for fun?''

''Isn't fun enjoyment? I enjoy working on the house.''

She shook her head in exasperation. ''Fun doesn't have a goal. It's just something that makes you laugh and relaxes you and has no purpose except to make you feel good.''

He thought about it for a few moments. ''I play poker once a month with some of the guys from the department.''

She waited, but when he didn't add anything else, she asked, ''That's it?''

''Entertainment's a little limited in Storkville.''

''But Omaha's less than an hour away. Do you date?''

''No.''

''Why not?''

''That's none of your business, Emma.'' He didn't want to get into that…not with her. A man dated for two reasons—to get his needs met or in the hopes that the dating would progress into something more. He wouldn't use a woman simply to meet a physical need, and he didn't want anything more.

Emma looked hurt by his blunt reply and leaned back against the booth, opening her menu.

An awkward silence fell over them and it lasted throughout supper. Emma commented on the good taste of the fried chicken. Tucker mentioned that the diner had great coconut cream pie. But neither of them ordered dessert. At the cash register Tucker paid their bill and after he received his change, Emma said, "We don't have to go to the movies, if you have something else you'd rather do."

He didn't have something else he'd rather do. That was the hell of it. He liked being with her. "A movie will be good for us both. What do you want to see? The theater here only has two screens, so we don't have much of a choice." Tucker mentioned the names of the two movies. One was full of gunfire and bombs, the other was purported to be a romantic comedy. They chose the romantic comedy.

But once inside the theater, Tucker felt as if he'd miscalculated on a lot of fronts. Only about ten people sat in the whole place, and there was an intimacy in the theater that might not have existed in a packed house. Tucker guided Emma to two seats in the middle of the center row. If they were going to have the place practically to themselves, they might as well pick the best vantage point.

Emma folded her coat on the seat next to her, and Tucker did the same with his jacket and hat. When they sank onto the cushioned seats, their arms brushed and they both moved away. Tucker sincerely hoped he could get engrossed in the movie so he'd forget about the woman beside him.

But forgetting didn't come easy, not when her perfume wafted toward him on a cold draft, not when she looked so delicate and exciting outlined in the shadows. He tried to concentrate on the characters on the screen and their dialogue, but he glanced at Emma often and felt a strange longing to hold her hand. What a ridiculous notion for a thirty-seven-year-old man who'd sown wild oats, gotten married, divorced and sworn off relationships!

His long legs didn't quite have enough room and after a while, he shifted. But his trouser leg brushed Emma's skirt, and the charge that jolted through him could have lit up all of Storkville. The few people in the audience laughed from time to time but Tucker was too distracted to let clever quips sink in. And when the couple on the screen had their first prolonged kiss, his shifting had nothing to do with his long legs.

The movie seemed never-ending. Finally the music swelled and the couple on the screen jet-setted into the sunset. Tucker breathed a sigh of relief. But when he looked over at Emma, he saw she was brushing a tear away.

"Are you okay?"

"I'm fine. I love happy endings."

"It's a shame they're not true to life," he murmured.

"You don't believe love conquers all?" Her eyes were wide with innocent curiosity.

"No. I believe we survive the best we can."

"Tucker!" she scolded. "Life is about more than surviving." A certainty in her soft voice enfolded his heart.

The lights went on in the theater and Tucker saw Emma's belief shining in her eyes. What would it be like not to have a past, to have a slate as clean as a field of fresh snow? Would Emma change when she remembered who she'd been? Or would she still have an ideal notion of the way the world should be?

Rather than responding, he stood, set his hat on his

head and shrugged on his jacket. Before she could protest, he lifted her coat and held it for her. With a murmured thanks, she slipped into it. His fingers lingered on
her collar under her hair. Such soft, silky hair. He could
imagine it spread across his pillow—

With a mental oath, he pushed up his seat and crossed
the aisle.

They walked to Tucker's truck in silence. At the passenger door, Emma looked up at the sky. It was a velvet
black, sprinkled with hundreds of stars. A crisp wind
blew her hair across her cheek. Tucker resisted the urge
to gently finger it, to brush it away, and he opened her
door.

Once he was seated beside her in the truck, he didn't
start the engine. Unlike the sheriff's SUV with the bucket
seats, his truck had bench seats and Emma was less than
six inches away. "Emma, in the restaurant, I didn't mean
to be so..."

"Blunt?" she filled in. "That's okay, Tucker. You're
right. Your life isn't any of my business. It's just hard
for me to remember that when we're living under the
same roof and when you know every...detail about me."

The way she said it, he knew she had something spe-
cific in mind and he could guess what it was. "Does it
bother you that I know you're a virgin?"

"No...yes...I don't know," she murmured as if she
was embarrassed by discussing it. "I think it makes you
look at me in a certain way, and that makes you think I
need your protection."

"Someone protected you before me, Emma. The doctor says he thinks you're in your early twenties. It's rare
nowadays for girls to be virgins past high school graduation." He shifted to face her more squarely. "I know
you belong to someone."

She shook her head. "You don't know anything of the sort, and neither do I. Sometimes in the middle of the night, I think about where I came from, and you know what I've decided?"

"What?"

"That maybe I was a princess kept hostage in a high tower and somehow I escaped and ran to Storkville, and now here I am."

In the glow of the parking lot lights, he could see her smile. Nothing in the world could keep him from brushing her hair away from her cheek, from leaning closer. "I wish I could believe in your version," he said, his voice husky.

"Believe it, Tucker." She raised her chin slightly and although he knew he shouldn't, he couldn't keep his lips from meeting hers.

Even though she'd told herself she wasn't expecting another kiss, and she shouldn't even *want* another kiss, she waited for Tucker and let the heat of his lips engulf her. There was so much heat in him, so much passion that swept through her as his tongue stroked hers.

Yet as easily as he'd bent to her, he abruptly pulled away. She wondered why...if he still thought another kiss was a mistake, until she became aware of voices and saw a couple approaching the truck on the driver's side. Tucker's lawman instincts must have alerted him.

As the couple passed Tucker's window, Emma recognized them. They had been sitting a few rows in front of her and Tucker inside the movie theater. The girl's hair was thick, auburn and straight, drifting down her back. It blew in the wind. Suddenly Emma's head started to pound. A pain lanced through her right temple, and she brought her hand up to it reflexively.

"Emma? What's wrong?"

She heard the murmur of Tucker's voice, yet not his words. She was lost somewhere, somewhere black that turned to gray and then a picture. She was brushing auburn hair and braiding it. The pain in her temple became worse and she saw herself tying a small blue bow on the end of the braid. Just as quickly as the vision had come, it vanished, and Emma felt breathless and shaken.

Tucker was clasping her arm now. "Emma, tell me what's happening."

"I saw...I saw something."

"That couple who passed by?"

"The woman...she...her hair—" She knew she wasn't making any sense and she tried to think past the throbbing in her head. "I got a headache and then, and then I was brushing someone's hair and braiding it. It was auburn, just like that girl's."

Tucker reached up to Emma's temples and massaged gently. "Did you see anything else?"

"A blue ribbon. I was tying a blue ribbon on the braid."

Tucker's voice remained steady and calm. "Can you see yourself? How old you are?"

"It's gone, Tucker. I can't see anything now."

His fingers were comforting and sensual and although her head still pounded, the pain was diminishing.

"See if you can get it back again."

She tried. She tried to see it once more. But she couldn't, and she shook her head.

Yet he kept probing. "How old were you?" he asked again.

"I...I don't know."

"Could you tell how old the girl was? Was she a child, a teenager?"

"Tucker, I don't know," she responded, frustrated

now. "I could only see her hair...my fingers on her braid...and the ribbon."

"Okay," he murmured, pulling her close to him, letting her head rest on his shoulder. "Try to relax. If you let your thoughts scatter, maybe it will come back."

She knew what he was thinking, that she was trying too hard to remember, that the harder she tried, the less she'd see. He was probably right. But her heart was still pounding, and her head hurt, and he felt so good and safe and strong as she leaned into him.

After he stroked her hair for a few moments, he leaned away. She looked up at him, wishing he'd kiss her again. But he didn't.

"Are you ready to go back to the house now? A good night's sleep might help, and maybe one of your headache pills."

She shook her head. "I don't like taking them. They make me feel...fuzzy."

"It won't hurt if you're fuzzy while you're sleeping," he said with a slip of a smile.

"I suppose not." She moved closer to the door on the passenger side. She should be thrilled she'd had another flashback, and she was, she supposed.

But she was disappointed that their kiss had been interrupted, and even more disappointed with Tucker's attitude toward it. It was as if it hadn't happened. It was as if he didn't want to get close to her.

Once they were back at Tucker's house, Emma went upstairs. Tucker always made the rounds at night, checking the locks on the doors, making sure everything was as secure as it was supposed to be. He'd told her most people didn't lock their doors in Storkville, but he'd brought habits with him from the big city that were hard to break.

Emma changed into her nightgown and robe, ones Gertie had provided, then listened for Tucker's footsteps. Soon she heard his boots on the stairs and she opened her door.

He stopped when he reached the second floor and saw her. "Did you remember something else?"

"No. I wanted to thank you for dinner and the movie."

"No thanks necessary. I enjoyed them, too."

"Did you?" she asked, studying him, looking for an indication as to how he felt about her.

Crossing to her, he stood very close. His gaze seemed to linger on the ruffled neck of her blue flannel nightgown peeking out from beneath the flannel robe. "Emma, about what I said at the diner…I'm a private person."

"But you told me about your childhood," she protested. After a few moments of silence when he didn't respond, she added, "It's just…I like you, Tucker."

"And I like you, too." He frowned. "That's the problem. You've got enough on your plate right now, and I'm not about to mess up anybody else's life."

It sounded as if he felt he'd done that once before, but before she could pursue it, he backed away from her. "Good night, Emma. I'll probably be gone before you're up in the morning."

"I'll be at the day-care center all day tomorrow."

He nodded and then went to his room and shut the door.

Emma's head still pounded but instead of taking one of the prescribed pills that made her feel a bit foggy in the morning, she took two acetaminophen. When she slipped into bed and turned off the light, she said a prayer, hoping that the flashback tonight had been an indication that she'd remember her life soon.

Once she remembered, then she could deal with her growing feelings for Tucker.

Chapter Three

The following evening, Tucker pulled into his garage, letting out a long breath. His day had gotten out of control. Earl had called in sick along with two other deputies so Tucker had taken the dayshift with Barry. Storkville was usually quiet and fairly crime-free. But today a mugger had struck again. Tucker guessed it was possibly the same one who'd stolen Emma's things. This time he'd snatched a purse from a teacher who had been walking home from school. Fortunately she was unharmed. Unfortunately, the man had worn a nylon stocking over his head again.

The day had rolled downhill from there. A few hours later he and Barry had covered a call at the Red Ball Tavern. The owner had phoned the department, fearing a fight was about to break out. Apparently a regular customer had too much to drink and accused a stranger of hustling him at pool. Tucker and Barry had sent the stranger on his way and taken the other man home. But from the belligerent attitudes of both men, Tucker suspected if they met up again, there could be further trouble.

And then there was coming home to Emma.

It was later than usual, about an hour and half later, but truth be told, he'd taken his time doing the paperwork on the mugging *and* the tavern call. Last night when he'd walked away from Emma's room, he'd wanted to turn around and take her into his arms. He'd wanted to kiss her and lead her to his bed. That desire was growing so strong, his self-restraint was wearing thin.

So he'd delayed coming home.

Coming home.

It *did* seem like a home with Emma here. Before that, it had simply been a house where he'd lived.

After he left the garage, he went to the kitchen. The lights were blazing, and he smelled the lingering aroma of food.

Emma came into the kitchen from the living room. "Hi. Are you okay?" She was wearing jeans and a soft blue sweater that begged to be touched. The gold necklace engraved with her name nestled above the round neckline of the sweater.

He hung up his jacket and hat. "I'm fine. Why wouldn't I be?"

"You're so late. I was afraid—"

"I had work to finish." His voice was gruffer than he intended because her concern unsettled him. If it *was* concern. He remembered all the arguments he'd had with Denise about his unusual hours.

Emma crossed to the oven and switched it off. "The roast beef is pretty dry, but I kept it warm. The mashed potatoes are stiff, but I can add milk and heat them up in the microwave if you'd like." As she moved to the refrigerator, she suggested, "Maybe the next time, you could call if you're going to be late."

He felt guilty for keeping her waiting, for worrying her, for ruining the supper she'd made. Since Chad's death, the guilt had plagued him, but during the past year or so, he'd kept it under the surface and manageable.

Now the look in Emma's eyes made him snap, "I'm not used to someone keeping tabs on me."

Her shoulders straightened, but her voice remained gentle. "That wasn't my intention. I'm just trying to repay your kindness."

Her quiet response unsettled him more. "Let's get something straight, Emma. You don't need to repay me in any way, and our lives are separate while you're staying here. You can go anywhere, do anything you want and so can I. As far as my hours, I never know when there might be an emergency, where I'll be, or what time I'll be home."

"In other words," her voice quivered slightly, "I shouldn't expect you for supper or at any other time of the day. And my life has nothing to do with yours except, of course, for the search for my identity."

When she put it into words, it made him sound callous and selfish, but that was better than him taking advantage of her or of wanting something he could never have. So he answered, "Exactly."

After a hard, steady stare, she tossed her hair over her shoulder. "Fine. Then you know where the food is, and I'll be in my room reading. Not that you need to know that, of course, but I thought it might be courteous of me to tell you."

She left him standing in the kitchen, his appetite turned to dust, his conscience telling him he'd not only offended her, but probably hurt her, too. Letting out an oath that would have turned Emma's face red, he opened the oven door and saw two plates covered with tinfoil. Loosening his string tie with it's State of Nebraska emblem, he tossed it onto the table and sighed. She hadn't eaten her supper, and now because of him, she probably wouldn't. After he opened the top two buttons of his shirt, he wrestled with the dilemma of what he should do. He didn't have to wrestle with it long...because he knew.

Fifteen minutes later, he'd filled two glasses with milk, found the old metal tray he used on poker nights to transport food from one place to the other, placed the warm plates on it, then carried the tray upstairs.

At the guest room door, he called, "Emma."

He heard her cross to the door and when she opened it, her eyes widened and his gut clenched. She was wearing that soft flannel nightgown and robe again.

"You didn't eat," he scolded her.

"I had breakfast and lunch today," she said with a touch of defiance that he hadn't noticed in her before.

"Three meals are better than two. You won't have any energy in the morning if you don't eat tonight."

She gave him a skeptical look. "Tucker, it's late. I'm really not hungry."

He'd never been very good at apologizing. "I didn't mean for you to worry tonight, Emma."

As she closely studied him, he felt she was trying to see down too deep. But he let her look, and he let her decide if she wanted to accept his apology or not.

"Should I come downstairs, or do you want to eat in here?" she asked softly.

"Will it bother you if we eat in your room?"

She slowly shook her head. "I trust you, Tucker."

He swallowed hard. He hoped to heaven he was worthy of that trust.

When she moved aside, he crossed to the bed and set the tray on it. Then he took a plate and sat in the rocking chair a few feet from the bed.

Emma propped two pillows against the headboard and settled there. They ate in silence for a few moments and then she asked, "Did you have a rough day today?"

He supposed it was an apt conclusion considering the way he'd acted. "I've had worse, but we think your mugger struck again. I don't like having somebody like that running around Storkville."

"Was someone hurt?"

"Fortunately, she wasn't," Tucker said.

"Could she describe him?" Emma asked.

"No. He wore a nylon stocking, just as he did when he mugged you. Aunt Gertie told us he was medium-size and this woman said the same thing. Unfortunately there are plenty of medium-size men around. I ran into a few at the Red Ball Tavern on my last call of the day."

"Aunt Gertie told me bikers hang out there."

"Not only bikers, but some local men who are down on their luck. Others just looking for a relaxing time…or trouble. But the bartender called us in when he thought a fight was going to break out."

"Did it?"

"No. Today we got there in time. Barry and I acted as a taxi service for one of the men. I felt sorry for him. He lost his job in the fall when the textile mill over in Cedarton closed. But he's got to realize sitting at the Red Ball drinking and betting on pool games isn't going to pay his mortgage."

Taking a sip of milk, Emma studied Tucker. "Do you take an interest in all your troublemakers?"

"I dealt with some real lowlifes in Chicago, but I also discovered people on the wrong side of the law because they didn't know better or weren't taught better or thought they had no other choice. When I could do something to change that, I tried.''

''You're a good man, Tucker.''

When she looked at him like that, he could almost believe her. She looked so adorable curled up on her bed, her lips moist from the milk. It would be so easy to go over and sit beside her, to kiss her and let desire take them where it would. But that would be wrong.

After he finished everything on his plate, he took it over to the bed and set it on the tray.

She did the same and stood before him, looking up at him. ''Thanks for bringing supper up. I was hungry after all.''

Her copper-red curls framed her face and lay enticingly on the ruffle of her nightgown. He fingered one of them. ''I'm not used to talking about my day with someone.''

''You can talk to me about your day anytime.''

She was such a good listener. She had a way of concentrating on him that made him feel as if he were the only person in the world, and nothing was more important than what he had to say. If he didn't get out of her room now, they'd both be sorry.

Letting her hair slip through his fingers, he backed away and picked up the tray. When he'd stepped over the threshold, he turned and gazed at her once more. ''The next time I'm going to be late, I'll try to call.'' When she smiled at him, he headed for the stairs. This woman was confusing his life.

But it was a confusion that felt good as well as uncomfortable, and that made no sense at all.

The weekend passed quickly. Emma wasn't surprised when Tucker went to the sheriff's department on Saturday. He put in long hours. But on Sunday when he disappeared and worked with drywall in the basement for most of the day, she was disappointed and felt he was avoiding her. Or maybe he was avoiding the sparks that always ignited between them when they got close. He came upstairs for supper when she called him, but then worked until bedtime.

Sometimes he acted like a confirmed bachelor... detached. But then others... She sensed the longing in him for more than what he had, for more than a house where he lived alone. His kindness and gentleness belied the tough-guy image he tried to project.

As usual, Emma went to the day-care center on Monday. After she and the day-care volunteers finished serving the children lunch, Emma gravitated toward Sammy and Steffie as she always did in a spare moment. The two adorable twins drew her and she wasn't sure why. She didn't want to miss any of their expressions, any of the new skills they were learning so quickly she could hardly keep up. She only knew she felt comfortable when she was with them and on the verge of knowing who she was. It was an odd feeling.

Emma sat on the floor with the twins on a quilt and entertained them with a Busy Box. When she pushed the lever, a dog face popped up and Steffie squealed and giggled in delight. When Emma turned a knob, a cat face appeared and Sammy reached for it. Aware of the ringing door chimes in the background, Emma kept her concentration on Sammy and Steffie.

A few moments later, she heard a male voice. It seemed...familiar.

When she looked up, she saw the back of a man in a denim jacket. His hair was blond and when he turned...

Emma's head began pounding. Her hands became clammy and then shook, and the world seemed to spin.

Aunt Gertie, who'd been hovering nearby and was picking up toys scattered on the floor, came over to Emma. "What's wrong, child? You're as white as one of my bleached sheets."

"I…" Emma was having trouble catching her breath, her heart was racing so fast. "I'm not sure. I…"

Recognition instantly flared in the man's eyes when he saw Emma sitting on the floor. He came toward her with a wide smile.

Emma's head felt as if it was going to explode and when he asked, "Emma, where have you been? I've been looking all over for you."

Cal. Cal Swenson.

Suddenly her world seemed to burst into amazing colors, into so many bright, shiny memories, she couldn't keep them all straight. One thought tumbled over the other. Then she looked down at Sammy and Steffie and knew why she felt comfortable with them. They were her niece and nephew!

"Emma. Talk to me, honey," Aunt Gertie said as she crouched down beside her.

"I remember! I remember everything. Sammy and Steffie are my niece and nephew, and I didn't know where Josie had taken them."

"Who's Josie?" Aunt Gertie asked.

"My sister. She lives with me. She told me she was taking the twins to the playground, and she left with them…and our car. She never came back. Then she left me a message on my answering machine a couple of days later."

Cal had gotten to Emma by then and scooped her up

into a huge bear hug. "It's good to see you're okay. What are you doing here? Did you decide on a new career?"

Aunt Gertie tapped Cal on the shoulder, and he let go of his hold on Emma.

"So what's your last name?" Aunt Gertie asked Emma.

"Douglas. I'm Emma Douglas," Emma responded happily. "I have to call Tucker."

Aunt Gertie looked up at Cal. "Emma got a nasty bump on the head and she's had amnesia. We didn't know who she was or where she came from, and I think right now she ought to sit down and rest for a few minutes until she absorbs all this."

Cal was looking stunned. Emma glanced down at the floor where she'd left Steffie and Sammy. Hannah was playing with them now, from her expression, she could see Hannah had overheard everything. Emma reminded herself Hannah officially had temporary custody of the twins.

"They live with me," she said softly to Hannah. "They're my sister's but..."

"We'll get it all straightened out," Hannah said. "Why don't you go upstairs with Gertie and lie down for a little while?"

"But I don't want to lie down. I..." Her head was still throbbing, and she took a deep breath to calm the trembling inside of her.

"You're still very pale," Aunt Gertie noticed. "There will be plenty of time to work all this out. Come on. After I get you settled, I'll call Tucker."

"Who's Tucker?" Cal wanted to know.

"He's the sheriff," Emma answered. "I've been...staying with him."

Cal's brows arched. "I'll stick around down here and

wait for him. You just give a yell if you need me. I'm not going anywhere until you tell me to. I figure you'll be wanting a ride back to Cedarton.''

Cedarton. Her home. Only about a half hour away. She'd left there in August and now it was November. And where was Josie?

Aunt Gertie's call to Tucker hit him like a ton of bricks. Emma had regained her memory and there was a tall blond man at the day-care center waiting to take her home. The hell he would! Not until Tucker knew exactly what had happened and what was going on.

He felt like putting on his siren on his way to BabyCare, but that would be foolish. There wasn't an emergency, just a mess that had to be untangled. Gertie had told him that Emma was Sammy and Steffie's aunt. Where was their mother? And who was their father?

Without ringing the bell, Tucker pushed open the door to BabyCare and hurried inside. Gertie immediately came into the small foyer.

''Where's Emma?'' he asked.

''I got her to lie down upstairs. Why don't you give her a few minutes? Hannah and the trucker who brought Emma to Storkville are in the kitchen.''

Trucker? The first thing Tucker wanted to find out was what this guy meant to Emma. Was he her boyfriend? Had she lived with him? No. It couldn't be. She was still a virgin.

It was time to put all of it in order.

When he entered the kitchen, both Hannah and the trucker looked up. She introduced the two men. ''Cal Swenson, Tucker Malone. Tucker, Cal's a friend of Emma's.''

Tucker gave the man a good once-over. He was about

five foot ten with scruffy good looks and an easy smile. He appeared to be about Emma's age.

After Tucker shook the man's hand, he said, "Aunt Gertie tells me you brought Emma to Storkville. Do you want to tell me about it?"

Cal shrugged. "There's not a lot to tell. Emma and her sister Josie live on a small farm in Cedarton. Their pop died right before Josie was born, and Emma pretty much helped raise her. When Emma was eighteen, her momma died, and she became legal guardian of Josie. They live on the farm and don't have a lot of outside contact. Emma's a computer whiz, designs Web sites and works out of the house. Since the twins were born about a year ago, she's been kept pretty busy."

"How old is her sister?"

"Josie's twenty now, but she's a flitterbug. Having the twins kind of overwhelmed her, I guess. She doesn't know what she wants to do or what she *should* be doing. So Emma's always taken responsibility for all of them."

After Tucker pulled out a chair, he sat across from Cal. "Where's Josie now?"

"That's why Emma came to Storkville," Cal explained. "Josie just up and disappeared with the twins. But then she called and left Emma a message two days later, saying she was doing the best thing for all of them and Emma shouldn't worry—that they were fine. But Emma does worry. All the time. She and Josie share an old car and Josie took off in it, so Emma was kinda stuck. She knew I was heading out to Los Angeles and asked me to bring her to Storkville so she could talk to people, have a look around, see if Josie had been here. It was early evening when I left her out at the gas station. She said she was going to stay at a bed and breakfast, then start her search in the morning.

"Why did you leave at night?"

"I like driving then."

"How was Emma going to get back to Cedarton?" Tucker pressed, wanting all of the answers.

"She said she'd find her own way back, even if she had to hire a cab. But I figured she'd be on a bus chasing after Josie as soon as she found out which direction her sister was headed. That girl and those twins mean everything to Emma."

"Why hasn't anyone missed Emma?" Tucker couldn't believe no one had reported her missing.

"Like I said, they kept pretty much to themselves. I've been on the west coast since August, taking trucking jobs out there. I got back a few days ago and went out to the farm. Newspapers were stacked high. I have a key to the house and tripped over a pile of mail the postman had dropped in the door slot. I looked around, but nothing was wrong except for all the messages on Emma's answering machine. I played them and some of the people had called two and three times about business, so I got worried."

"How did you know Emma was here?"

"I didn't. I stopped in at the General Store and asked some questions. The clerk there said a woman had turned up, nobody knew who she was, and she volunteered down here most days."

There was silence for a few moments until Tucker pushed himself away from the table and stood. "So you and Emma are friends?"

"Sure are. Have been for about five years. Ever since I moved to this area."

Five years. That was a long friendship and maybe more. But Tucker knew that was none of his business, or at least that's what he told himself. "Did anyone call Emma's doctor?" Tucker asked Hannah.

"I offered to, but she said it wasn't necessary."

"We'll see about that," he mumbled as he headed for the stairs.

When Tucker found Emma in a small room on the second floor, she wasn't resting on the bed, but rather standing at the window looking out. She turned at the sound of his bootsteps and asked, "Did Aunt Gertie tell you I remember everything?"

"I just had a talk with Swenson. But before we get into all that, how do you feel? Shouldn't you call your doctor?"

She shook her head. "I still have a bit of a headache, but it's fading. I need to put all of this in perspective. I need to figure out what I'm going to do. I've got to find Josie."

The beautiful woman before him had her memory back now. As he studied her, he looked for signs that her memory had caused changes, had turned her into someone else. But he couldn't find them. She still looked vulnerable and innocent and apparently her thoughts were for her sister, not for what she herself had been through the past two months.

Crossing to her, he gently clasped her elbow and guided her to a rocking chair. "Let's talk about your sister," he said as he sat on the edge of the bed across from her, his knees almost touching hers.

"How much trouble is she in?" Emma asked, her eyes pleading with him to tell her everything would be all right.

Abandonment went through Tucker's mind. "Let's take this one step at a time. Why do you think your sister left the twins at BabyCare and not with you?"

There was pain in Emma's eyes. "In her message, she told me she wanted me to be free to live my own life. I think she's always felt like a burden and didn't know what to do about it. Our mother worked long hours as a secretary and she expected me to take care of Josie. When she died, Josie was thirteen and it was just the two of us."

Doing some quick calculations, Tucker figured Emma was twenty-five. Apparently she'd had more responsibility than she'd needed most of her life. Had the amnesia been a way of her taking a break from that? "Certainly she knew how you felt about the twins."

"I thought she did, but maybe she didn't. Maybe she thought that I considered them a burden, too."

"Did Josie work?"

"Yes. Mostly temporary jobs, though, because she really doesn't have any skills."

"Why did you think she was in Storkville?"

"Because I found a matchbook advertising the General Store with a man's name inside."

"Anything else? A number?"

"No. She'd just drawn a little heart with the name Josie and Jack written through it."

"Do you think he's the babies' father?"

"I don't know. She wouldn't tell me anything about the father." Emma bit her lower lip. "What's going to happen with the twins? Hannah has temporary custody, and she's so fond of them. But I've practically raised them and I love them."

Although he'd tried to stay objective and impersonal, now he took Emma's hand between his two, and his objectivity vanished in the wake of the worry in her eyes. "*You* are their closest relative right now. And yes, Hannah's fond of them, but she knew her custody order was temporary. Certainly she'll want to see them happy and back where they belong. Every time you're with them, it's obvious that they belong with you. We'll have to call Health and Human Services and unravel all the red tape. Maybe I can smooth the way. I won't know how long the unravelling will take until I talk with them.''

Emma's eyes filled with tears and Tucker asked gently, ''What's wrong?''

''I never realized how isolated we were on the farm. I never realized what it was like being part of a community, having people around who care about you. I always had Josie and then Cal. But these last two months with you and Aunt Gertie, Gwen, Hannah and everybody here, I've almost felt like I had a larger family.''

Tucker knew exactly what Emma was getting at. He was pretty sure she was going to say that she should go back home. But he wasn't certain that was the best thing for her, or for the twins. ''I don't think you should move too fast right now. We're going to call your doctor. I want you to talk to him. I don't think you should be alone somewhere. As for the twins, well, as you said, there are a lot of people here who care about them. It might be easier for Hannah to let go of them if she could still see them now and then. I'm sure Gertie can help you out with them. If you're living with me, you'll be nearby everyone...''

''Living with you?''

''Just till we get the whole situation untangled. Once I have Josie's Social Security number, birth date and your license plate number, it shouldn't take too long to find her.''

''Really?''

''Unless she doesn't want to be found. Then it might

take us a little longer. But in the meantime, you'll have people around you who care.''

''You've no idea what it's like taking care of twins or the chaos they can cause. Are you sure you want that in your house?''

Because of his work, he hadn't been around much when Chad was a baby. Maybe somehow he saw helping Emma and the babies she loved as a way to make up for his past sins. He didn't know. He didn't know how he'd feel being around the twins. But his gut instinct told him he shouldn't let her leave yet.

''That's exactly why you should stay,'' he pointed out. ''But I should take you to Cedarton, so you can get me a picture of Josie and the information we need. Health and Human Services will want the babies' birth certificates and proof of your identity.''

''I'd finished outstanding projects before I came to Storkville, but I've got to pay the bills, check on work that's come in and call lots of people who probably wonder what happened to me.''

Tucker stood. ''The first thing we're going to do is call your doctor.''

''Tucker…''

''Humor me, Emma.''

She seemed to stop and take stock, and after a look at his face, she smiled. ''All right. But if you want to get back to work, Cal can take me to Cedarton.''

Tucker didn't like that idea at all. ''I think it's better if I go with you. I can look around and figure out what might help me best in the investigation.''

Emma nodded. ''All right.'' Then she grinned at him. ''Tucker, I remember who I am! I have my life back.''

But then the grin slipped away. "Now if we can just find Josie…"

"We'll find her, Emma. I promise you we will." When he did, there would be a reckoning with the young woman who had put Emma through this hell.

Chapter Four

After Tucker drove down a long lane bordered with pines, he pulled up in front of the house where Emma had grown up. He studied the old farmhouse with its white siding and burgundy shutters. The white barn, a few hundred yards away, needed a coat of paint.

"How big is the farm?" Tucker asked.

"About twenty acres. But we lease out the land for its income."

They hadn't talked much on the drive to Cedarton. When Emma had called Dr. Weisensale, he'd insisted she come in immediately. It had been hard for Emma to drag herself away from Sammy and Steffie. Although she'd spent time with them over the past two months, she'd missed being their primary caretaker. Her love for them made her want to take them into her arms and hold on tightly forever. But she'd left them with Hannah, worried about what was going to happen next.

Dr. Weisensale had given Emma a clean bill of health, just warned her not to overdo things and try to keep stress to a minimum. Keep stress to a minimum with not knowing what was going to happen with the twins, with not knowing if her sister would ever be found.

With Tucker by her side, Emma walked up the wooden porch steps and took out the spare key Cal had had in his possession. He'd wanted to bring her home himself, but she'd explained that there were things Tucker needed and it was better if he went to the farm with her. Cal had assured Emma he'd keep in close touch and watch over the farm for her. She should let him know if she needed anything because he'd be around until after Christmas, driving locally.

Opening the screen door for Emma, Tucker stood aside while she put the key in the lock and pushed open the door.

Everything was as she'd left it except for the stacks of mail on the dining room table and over two months worth of newspapers sitting beside them. It was cold in the house and she shivered. The furnace had been off when she left in late summer and Cal had only turned it on high enough that the pipes wouldn't freeze.

Tucker took it all in, from the worn couch and armchairs, to the scarred dining room table, to Emma's computer workstation lodged in one corner.

Going to the bookshelves in the living room, Emma gathered up two framed pictures of Josie. The first was her sister's high school graduation picture. The second was more recent, a photo of her and the twins in the backyard on a blanket. Emma had had it enlarged from a snapshot in June.

As Tucker went into the dining room, she took them from their frames, then crossed to him. "This is my sister," she said softly.

Studying the pictures closely, he assured her, "This

will be a good start. I already called in her Social Security number, birth date and your license plate number while you were seeing the doctor. Do you have any credit cards she might use?''

Emma went to a rolltop desk near her workstation, took out a paid bill from one of the slots, and handed it to him. He laid it on the table with the snapshots.

''The twins' birth certificates are in a strongbox upstairs. I'll get them and pack some of my clothes and a few of their favorite toys. Unless... Tucker, are you sure you want me to stay with you?''

''I think that would be best until we get this situation with the twins ironed out, don't you? You can't get back and forth without a car, and I'm sure you're going to want to see them every day.''

He was right about all of it. Only one thing troubled her. ''I can access my phone messages from Storkville, but what if Josie comes home?''

''Leave a note for her and tell her you're staying with me.''

Whenever Tucker spoke of Josie, there was a hardness in his voice that made Emma uneasy. She remembered what he'd said about his mother abandoning him and his father, and he probably saw Josie as a woman in the same light. But he didn't know her. He didn't realize how sweet and how just plain young she was. Her main problem had always been her impulsiveness. In a convoluted way, Josie probably thought she was doing the best thing for the twins, leaving them at the day-care center. Storkville had such a wonderful reputation for its care of children that she'd known they'd be well taken care of. Trying to put herself in her sister's shoes, she could understand how Josie might think she was lifting a burden from Emma. But Emma had never seen Josie and the twins as a burden. They were her family and she'd do anything for them.

"I'll write a note and leave it on the refrigerator. That's where she'll look first if I'm not here."

Tucker motioned to the mail on the table. "Why don't I put all that in a bag and we'll take it with us. Then you won't have to hurry through it."

He was being so thoughtful, she felt tears come to her eyes. But she hurriedly blinked them away. "Thank you. I won't be long."

She hadn't intended to take long, but after she went upstairs to the linen closet and took the twins' birth certificates from the strongbox, she stopped in Josie's room. It still looked like the room of a teenager, really, with its stuffed animals, scrapbooks, the poster of a handsome pop star on the wall. So many questions assaulted Emma. What had happened that Josie felt she had had to leave? That she couldn't cope? That she had to make a life on her own? It was painful standing in Josie's room, and Emma moved on to the nursery.

The two cribs with their mobiles swinging above them, blue-and-pink striped wallpaper, the changing table with its stack of diapers beside it, comforted Emma for a moment until she realized the twins weren't in her custody yet. Tucker had called Health and Human Services, and he and Emma were meeting with the caseworker tomorrow morning. But if the authorities decided the twins should stay in Hannah's custody…

Emma wrapped her arms around herself, staring at the toys, the animals, everything that babies needed.

"Emma." The deep vibration of Tucker's voice ran through her, and she turned to face him. When he saw her expression, he came into the room. "What is it?"

"What if I lose them? What if somebody decides I'm not fit to be a mother?"

Tucker's strong arms enfolded Emma close to him and he rested his chin on top of her head. "I can't tell you you're worrying needlessly, but from everything you've told me, no one is better fit to be a mother after taking care of Josie all these years, and then her *and* the twins."

"But I don't have any family to stand up for me. Cal's the only one who's seen me with Josie and the twins. They're all I have, Tucker," she said in a trembling voice. "Especially if we can't find Josie."

When he tipped her face up to his, he suggested, "How about if we take this one step at a time? I'll stand up for you, and Gertie will, and even Hannah. She might be fond of the twins, but she knows they're not hers. And all of us have seen you with the children at the day-care center as well as with Sammy and Steffie."

"What if the father comes forward?" Emma asked, that worry as strong as any of the others.

"You think he's from Storkville?"

"I don't know what to think. No man has set foot near Josie since she's had the babies. Before that, I don't know where she spent time with a man or when. The months before she told me she was pregnant, she seemed exceedingly happy. That's when she was working at the McCormack estate."

"She must have taken the rattle I found with the babies from there."

"Josie wouldn't steal," Emma said with certainty.

"You're so sure of that?"

"It was an heirloom, Tucker. It had to mean something to her, or to the man who fathered her children."

He shook his head. "Well, Quentin McCormack's not the father. His DNA test ruled that out. The butler at the estate is supposed to return any time now. I'll talk to him when he does. Hopefully he'll remember Josie and maybe whoever she kept company with. But for now, I don't think you have to worry about the father. Everyone in Storkville has known about those babies and nobody has come forward.''

When Emma looked up at Tucker, she realized that when she was with him, everything seemed better. That was so odd since she'd been on her own so much of her life. She'd never depended on *anyone,* and she was hesitant to start now.

Taking her face between his hands, he murmured, ''It *will* all work out, Emma.''

She longed for him to prove that to her, and that longing must have shone in her eyes. He hesitated only a moment, then covered her lips with his. The erotic distraction of his kiss didn't make her worries vanish, but somehow Tucker holding her like this, kissing her, wanting her, made all of it seem more manageable. She gave back to him as best she could within her limited experience, touching her tongue to his bottom lip. When he groaned, he held her tighter. The fire that had burned between them since the night they'd met threatened to burst through its confines. But once again, Tucker was the one who doused it.

Tearing his lips from hers, he dropped his hands to his sides. He was breathing fast and heavy and so was she. ''The last thing we need is to make this more complicated.''

She supposed he was right, and yet her feelings for Tucker were the only thing that didn't seem complicated. They were growing deeper and deeper, day by day.

''Come on,'' he said gruffly. ''I want to look through Josie's room, if that's okay with you, to see if I can find any other clues. Then I want to get information about her into the computer. I just wish we had that new scanner we requisitioned.''

''I have a scanner. I can put the pictures on a disk or e-mail them to your address.''

His smile was slow but steady in coming. ''I forgot you were a computer whiz.''

''Not a whiz, just computer literate.''

''Swenson said you run your own business from here.''

''I design Web sites. Before we leave, I have to listen to the messages on the machine. Those are the first calls I'll have to make.'' Looking down at her hands, she realized she still held the two birth certificates. She gave them to Tucker.

After he took them, he folded them and stuffed them into his shirt pocket. ''We'll get everything straightened out, Emma. It's just going to take a little time.''

She'd lost two months of her life, two months of looking for Josie. Yet in that time she'd found Tucker and Aunt Gertie and everyone else in Storkville who had been so kind to her. Life took strange twists and turns. She just hoped the next turn would be one that would bring her joy instead of sadness.

When Tucker's doorbell rang at ten o'clock the following morning, Emma felt as if she was going to jump out of her skin. She'd made coffee and brownies and hoped that wouldn't be looked on as a bribe. Checking Tucker's living room, with its green-and-tan plaid couch and armchair, Boston rocker, and entertainment center, she saw everything was tidy.

When Tucker opened the door, a brunette in her forties

with a briefcase walked in and shook his hand. "Hello, Sheriff Malone."

After Tucker introduced Miss Brimswell to Emma, they all sat in the living room. Emma asked her if she'd like a cup of coffee, but the caseworker declined without smiling. Emma settled in the armchair and clasped her hands in her lap. She'd never been more nervous in her life.

From her position in the rocker, Mary Brimswell looked first at Emma, then at Tucker. "I'll tell you up front that we already have an unusual situation here. So please bear with me if I ask questions that might seem personal or even irrelevant."

"I'll answer anything you want to know," Emma said sincerely.

"That'll be a good start," the woman replied, this time with a small smile, as she opened her briefcase and removed a yellow legal pad and a pen. "You're the young lady who arrived in Storkville around the same time as the twins. But I understand you've had amnesia."

"That's right," Emma answered.

"Sheriff Malone tells me you've completely recovered from that."

"Yes, I have. I remember everything now—past and present."

The caseworker made notes on her pad. "I'd like the name of your doctor. And I have a release form for you to sign so that we can look at your records. Is that acceptable to you?"

"That's fine." The business-like tone in Mary Brimswell's voice worried Emma. "Miss Brimswell, I know that this is just another case to you, but the twins are my life."

"Yes, you claim to be their aunt," Mary Brimswell

responded. "Sheriff Malone told me yesterday you would have their birth certificates and personal identification."

Prepared, Emma took a file folder with the papers from the table next to her chair and handed them to the caseworker. "My purse was stolen and I'll have to replace my driver's license, but I had my voter registration card at home. I've also supplied you with a copy of last year's tax records. There's a picture of Josie and me with the twins in the folder, as well as a picture of our house. My doctor's name is there, too, along with character references and other information you might need."

The caseworker handed Emma the release form to sign as she sifted through the papers in the folder. "You've been very thorough. This will save us time." Setting the folder aside on the coffee table, she requested, "Now tell me about your life with the twins and Josie Douglas."

Beginning with the death of her father before Josie was born, Emma recounted how she'd taken care of Josie while her mother worked, and how she'd become her legal guardian after their mother died. Then she explained how she was able to work at home and help Josie take care of the twins after they were born.

"Did you *help* your sister, or were you their primary caregiver?"

Emma remembered how scared Josie had been when they'd learned she was having twins, how fatigued and uncertain she'd seemed after their birth. Knowing she had to tell the caseworker the truth, Emma admitted, "Josie was overwhelmed after the twins were born, so I did most of it. But she loves them dearly. She's just young and inexperienced and impulsive sometimes."

Apparently intent on taking comprehensive notes, Mary Brimswell was writing furiously. "I see. Well, with your sister missing, and no father in the picture, you *are* their closest living relative. The fact that you've been spending time with Sammy and Steffie at the day-care center, even though you didn't know you were related to them, has surely been good for them. Will you be returning to your home in Cedarton?''

"Tucker...Sheriff Malone...has invited me to stay here for a few weeks. He thinks he'll be able to find Josie. And it's not only that," Emma went on in a rush. "But Sammy and Steffie have gotten used to Aunt Gertie and Hannah and everyone at the day-care center."

The caseworker looked at Tucker. "You're willing to bring the twins into your home?''

His expression was serious. "Yes."

Mary Brimswell again looked from Tucker to Emma. "And what is your relationship to each other?''

"We're friends," Emma answered quickly.

"Is that the way you'd assess your relationship, Sheriff Malone?''

"Yes, it is."

"I know you're going to think this is none of my business, but the twins' welfare *is* my business. Are you sleeping together?''

Emma's and Tucker's voices chorused the word "No!" at the same time.

Picking up the folder Emma had given her, Mary Brimswell tucked it into her briefcase. "As I said, these are unusual circumstances. Fortunately, Sheriff Malone has a sterling reputation in this community and his help to you should be seen as an asset rather than a hindrance. From a cursory look at all this, I can say I will be recommending the judge transfer custody of Sammy and Steffie Douglas to you, Emma. But we'll have to go through the formality of a hearing. I'll try to set it up with a judge as soon as possible. I'm sure he'll be assigning a lawyer to the children to protect their interests. Do you have a lawyer?''

"No," Emma answered, glancing at Tucker. "Is one necessary? If Hannah's not contesting the change of custody…"

"She's not," the caseworker responded. "She thinks very highly of you, and she has chosen *not* to hire a lawyer. But you should have one there to present your case for you."

"I know a lawyer who handles family cases," Tucker said. "I'll call her and see if she'll meet with us as a favor to me."

"I'll pay her," Emma said firmly.

"We'll discuss it," he returned easily, and Emma knew he expected to get his way. They'd see about that.

Miss Brimswell asked if she could take a tour of the house. She wanted to see the room where the twins would be sleeping. Letting Tucker act as guide, Emma tried to stay calm.

Finally Miss Brimswell was ready to leave. After Tucker helped the caseworker with her coat, she picked up her briefcase and smiled at both of them. "I know this can be quite an ordeal, but we should have it over with fairly quickly."

"I can still see the twins until we meet with the judge, can't I?" Emma asked.

"That's not a problem. I spoke with Hannah Caldwell before I came over here. She understands the situation. Just give her a call beforehand."

After Tucker had closed the door behind Mary Brimswell, he turned to Emma. "You made a good impression," he said.

With a sigh of relief, Emma tried to relax. "How could you tell?"

He chuckled. "I've worked with Mary before. She doesn't say what she doesn't mean. If she thinks this will go smoothly, then it will. She has a lot of influence with the judge. Do you want to drive to Cedarton and get the cribs and whatever else you need for the babies?"

"I hate to run you up there again."

He shrugged. "I don't mind. I'm taking the day off. Unless there's a crisis somewhere I have to handle, I'm free. We can get the guest room upstairs ready."

"I'd like to do that. I'd also like to take a baby present I bought for Gwen Crowe out to her at the ranch. I missed her shower last night."

"Let's get everything from Cedarton first, then you can decide what you want to do next."

What she wanted to do next was throw her arms around Tucker's neck and give him a big thank-you kiss. But she was afraid she might shock him. So instead, she crossed to him and said, "Thank you, Tucker, for everything you're doing. It means a lot to me."

His gaze held hers for a few long moments. "It means a lot to me, too," he said hoarsely, and then breaking the silence that was becoming more intimate, he nodded toward the kitchen. "I'll call the lawyer. While I do, why don't you wrap up the brownies. We can eat them on the drive."

As Emma followed Tucker into the kitchen, she thought about the friendship that had grown between them. For her there was more. Did Tucker feel more, too? Or did he think friendship was enough?

That evening, Emma went upstairs to her room to get the present she'd bought for Gwen. She stopped in the doorway, letting her gaze pass over the cribs that Tucker had set up after their trip to Cedarton, the stacks of diapers, the baby monitor. Going over to one crib, she tapped the bear on the colorful mobile. After they'd come back from the farmhouse with all the baby paraphernalia, they'd gone to the day-care center to visit the twins. At least she had. Tucker had kept his distance from Sammy and Steffie, though there had been emotion in his eyes when he watched her play with them. She wished he'd tell her what was going on in his head, why he had invited her and the twins to stay with him.

Taking the gaily wrapped present from her closet, Emma returned downstairs. Tucker was waiting for her. He wore jeans and a navy-and-red flannel shirt, topped by a black insulated vest. He was so tall, so broad-shouldered, so thoroughly male, and as sexy out of uniform as in one.

"All set," she said as she took her coat from the closet.

"There was a message from Mary Brimswell when we got back. We're meeting with the judge Friday morning at eleven. There was also a message from the lawyer I called, Sandra Travis. She said she'd be glad to meet with you tomorrow. She has some time in the afternoon and you should call her around nine. She said she'll be glad to do this pro bono."

"I'm going to pay her fee." After they returned from their visit with the twins, Emma had filed for a replacement driver's license. Then, back at Tucker's, she'd paid bills, some of which were overdue, and contacted clients. There had been charges on her stolen credit card that she hadn't made—from a grocery store. The credit card company, as well as Tucker, were checking them. They'd also brought her computer back with them from Cedarton, and Tucker had set it up on a cardtable in his den. She needed to keep income rolling in.

"I knew you'd say that," he grumbled in response. "I guess you'll have to discuss it with Sandra." Gesturing to the garage, he asked, "Do you want to drive the pickup out to the Crowes' place?"

She zippered the green, down parka she'd brought from the farm and picked up the present. "Are you serious?"

"Sure. It just sits in the garage all day. If you need it to run errands, you'll be used to driving it."

"I'd like that. I should think about getting another car."

"There'll be time enough for that," he said.

Tucker's truck was easy to handle, but Emma concentrated on her driving as he gave her directions to Ben and Gwen's place. As she drove down the gravel lane to the ranch, the dark night hiding most of the scenery, Tucker informed her, "While you were playing with the twins, I showed Jackson Caldwell the picture of your sister and asked him if he'd ever seen her or dated her."

Jackson. Jack. The name that had been inside the matchbook cover. "Did he know her?"

"He says not, and he couldn't be the twins' father anyway. He just came back to Storkville when his father died six months ago."

"I guess we could go through the phone book and check out every Jack in town."

"If it comes to that, that's what I'll do," Tucker concluded as if he'd already thought of it. "The problem is, even if we find the man Josie was seeing, that doesn't mean he'll know where she is now."

"No. And if we find him…he might want his children. What if Josie didn't even tell him about them?"

"You'll drive yourself nuts *what-iffing*, Emma. Believe me, I know. Hopefully on Friday the judge will give you the twins. Then we'll proceed from there.''

Emma parked the pickup in front of a two-story ranch house, then she and Tucker went up the front steps and knocked on the door.

Wind blew across the porch, and Emma shivered. Cold weather was moving in early this year.

Gwen opened the door, looking tired. Still, she had a wide smile for them. ''Hi there. I hear you got your memory back yesterday. I'm so happy for you. How are you?''

''I'm fine. I'm sorry I had to miss your shower.'' She offered the present to Gwen. ''I wanted to give you this for the baby.''

''Come on in,'' Gwen said, motioning them inside. ''The place is still a mess. Ben went over to the school with Nathan to pick up his science project. He won honorable mention. We're so proud of him.''

There were boxes stacked here and there in the living room, and Gwen shook her head. ''I don't know if I'll ever get unpacked.'' She rubbed the small of her back. ''And with the baby coming anytime, disorder might be the order of the day.'' Her expression suddenly changed and she winced.

''Are you okay?'' Emma asked.

''I'm fine. Just a twinge in my back. Too much packing and unpacking.'' She looked down at the present. ''I just love opening gifts. But first, let me get you something to drink. Tucker, how about a cup of coffee?''

''Sounds good,'' he said with a smile.

But as Gwen started off toward the kitchen, she suddenly stopped, dropped the present and grabbed on to the doorjamb, letting out a loud, ''Oh.''

Emma rushed over to her. ''What's the matter?''

Gwen's eyes were wide as she gasped, "My water broke. I'm…I think I'm going to have this baby now."

Just then she doubled over and Tucker hurried to her, also. "We've got to get you to the hospital."

"I'm not going anywhere until Ben comes home."

"Gwen," Emma protested. "You don't know how much time you have."

Gwen held up her hand as she panted through the contraction. "Ben and I…are going to do…this together and I'm not going anyplace without him."

Tucker and Emma exchanged a look.

"At least, let me get you to the sofa," Tucker said as he put an arm around her waist and supported her.

Giving him a grateful smile, she nodded. "That would probably be a good idea."

"I'll try to call the school," Emma said.

But Tucker shook his head. "I'll do that. You stay here with Gwen."

Before he could move, another contraction ripped through Gwen, and Emma knelt beside her at the couch. "Gwen, you've got to let us take you to the hospital. That was only about two minutes since the last one."

"Ben will be back any minute. I know he will. I'm not leaving here without him."

"Stubborn woman," Tucker mumbled. "Are you prepared to have your baby here if he doesn't get back in time?"

"Having a child is a perfectly natural experience. It might be better to have my baby here without the sterility of a hospital."

Tucker came over to Gwen and peered down at her. "Sterility can be a good thing, Gwen. I'm going to call an ambulance."

"Don't you dare. If you call an ambulance, Tucker Malone, I won't vote for you in the next election."

At that, he just shook his head in amazement.

"We need to get a few things together, Tucker, just in case," Emma told him. "Can you boil some water? Put a pair of scissors in it and string if you can find it."

"I feel like I have to push, Emma. What should I do?" Gwen asked her.

Just then, there was a sound of tires on the gravel outside, and Tucker hurried to the door. "It's Ben and Nathan."

When Ben came in, he took one look at his wife and rushed to her side. "You weren't supposed to start without me."

"Tell that to the baby," she murmured as her face twisted in pain. She bit down on her lip, hard.

"She wouldn't let me call an ambulance," Tucker told Ben.

Gwen clutched her husband's arm. "We won't make it to the hospital. I just know it. Emma said she can help."

Before any of them could move a muscle, Ben knelt down beside his wife.

Gwen gazed at him. "I want to have the baby here in our home."

"Honey, that's a fine idea, but I don't want to take any chances and you don't either, do you?"

She looked at him with all the love she felt for him. "No, I guess not, but still…"

"I'll call an ambulance and if they're here in time, fine. If not, they'll be here to check you out. Okay?" He covered her hand with his.

"Okay," she nodded.

Going to the phone, Tucker said, "I'll make the call."

The next few minutes were a scurry of activity as Ben stayed with his wife, and Emma went upstairs to find a sheet and some towels.

Nathan stood at Ben's side taking it all in until Ben put his arm around the boy. "You're going to have a brother or sister soon."

"Is Gwen going to be okay?"

There was perspiration on Gwen's face as she panted through another contraction.

Ben said to Nathan, "Having a baby is hard work. She'll be fine. Why don't you go out to the kitchen with Tucker."

After Nathan did as Ben suggested, Emma laid towels under Gwen on the sofa and then covered her with a sheet. By that time, they heard the squeal of a siren, but Gwen moaned, "I have to push, Emma. Can you look?"

Emma had been Josie's coach throughout her pregnancy and during her labor and delivery. She'd paid attention very carefully in case this exact same thing had happened to Josie and they'd been stranded at the farmhouse. But Josie's labor had been long and they'd had plenty of time to get to the hospital.

Now as Emma checked Gwen, she said, "I can see the head. The next push, Gwen, give it all you've got."

Tucker's heart pounded hard as he watched the drama unfolding before him from the kitchen doorway. He'd missed the birth of his son. He'd been working on a case. As Denise had said afterwards, *What else was new?* But his overwhelming joy in Chad, his proud enthusiasm in being a father, had soothed their marriage for a time and made things better between them. But only for a time.

The odd thing was, as he watched Gwen and the miracle happening before his eyes, he was thinking about Emma. He was seeing her swollen with child...his child.

He couldn't shake the picture, and even when Nathan slid by him and stood watching too, Tucker stood immobilized.

There was a rap on the door and paramedics rushed in just as Emma caught the beautiful child and said to Gwen, "You have a lovely, lovely baby girl." As the baby let out her first cry, Ben kissed Gwen, and there were tears running down both their cheeks. When Nathan went over to the couple, they included him in their hug. Emma laid the baby in Gwen's arms.

The first paramedic said, "I don't think they need us." Then they took over anyway.

"I don't want to go to the hospital," Gwen reminded everyone as she looked down at her newborn. "Do I have to?"

The paramedic looked at Tucker. "I'll call the hospital." Then he took out his mobile phone while the other paramedic took the baby from Gwen, checking vital signs and her breathing.

An ache constricted Tucker's chest. It was so bad, he had to turn away and go back into the kitchen. He'd lost his son due to his job. He'd lost his wife because he'd failed as a husband.

He was still lost in the past when Emma came in and stood beside him. "They named her McKenna."

He was silent.

"I'd stay for a while and help, but Gwen seems to want to be alone with Ben and Nathan."

"She and the baby are okay?"

"The paramedics checked her out and consulted with the doctor. They're not going to take her to the hospital."

Tucker raked his hand through his hair. "We might as well get out of their way."

Although Emma studied him intently, she didn't ask any of the questions that were in her eyes, and he was grateful. He couldn't tell her about Chad. Not now.

Maybe not ever.

Chapter Five

Judge Martin Peabody sat behind a massive desk in his black robe on Friday morning, looking down his narrow nose, first at Steffie who was wriggling in Hannah's arms and then at Sammy, squirming in Jackson Caldwell's. "Let them down on the floor," he commanded.

Emma took a deep breath. For the past few days, she'd been on pins and needles about this meeting. She and Tucker sat on one side of the room with Mary Brimswell between them and Hannah and Jackson. At the judge's request, the two lawyers sat in the back after their preliminary presentation.

Now as the twins hit the ground, which in this case was an expensive oriental rug, they stopped fussing. Unmindful of that, they both crawled toward Emma as fast as their little legs could take them. When Sammy reached her, he used her black pants leg to pull himself up and smiled at her gleefully at his accomplishment. Steffie just sat at her feet, her arms raised, wanting to be picked up.

Judge Peabody took it all in. "It looks as if they gravitate toward you."

"Yes, sir." Not knowing what else to say, she gathered Steffie into her arms and put her on her lap.

The judge looked at Mary Brimswell. "I see what you mean. Maybe she forgot *them,* but they never forgot *her.*"

Tucker cleared his throat. "As Miss Travis pointed out, Emma spent a lot of time with the twins at the day-care center, even when she didn't know consciously that she was their aunt."

"I heard Miss Travis, Sheriff Malone. But I wanted to see for myself, and now I have. Miss Douglas, are you willing to take responsibility for your niece and nephew?"

Again she answered, "Yes, sir."

"Talk to me, Miss Douglas. Tell me why these two children belong with you."

Knowing this could be one of the most important moments of her life, all Emma could do was speak from her heart. "They belong with me, Your Honor, because I love them and my sister deeply. When she told me she was pregnant, I had no illusions about taking on the responsibility of a child because I had taken responsibility for her, even before my mother died. I coached Josie through labor, and I was with her when Sammy and Steffie were born."

She reflexively passed her hand up and down Steffie's back. "I've loved them as if they were my own since they were born. Maybe with one baby Josie would have taken full care and I could have removed myself a little. But with twins, she needed both my hands as well as hers—for feedings, for diapering, and for the affection they needed. I love them, Your Honor, and until Josie comes back..." She stopped, her voice catching.

"What if your sister doesn't return, Miss Douglas? Then what?"

Emma raised her gaze to his. "I have to believe she's safe. I have to believe she *will* come back. But practically speaking, I will give the twins everything a parent can give a child...as long as I need to."

After he shuffled through a few papers on his desk, Judge Peabody looked up at Emma. "In a very short amount of time, Miss Brimswell has managed to obtain quite a few character references for you. From Tucker Malone, Dana McCormack, Gertrude Anderson, Cal Swenson, Gwenyth Crowe, as well as Hannah Caldwell. Mrs. Caldwell's carries a considerable amount of weight since Miss Brimswell told me she entertained the idea of adopting the babies herself." He cast his attention on Hannah. "I admire your integrity in this matter. You could have made all of this very difficult."

"I want what's best for Sammy and Steffie," Hannah responded. "Seeing them with Emma, I know what that is."

He nodded. "Very well, then. Miss Douglas, I'm a cautious man, so this is what I'm going to do. I'm going to grant you custody for a period of three months—or until your sister returns. During that time, Miss Brimswell will visit you intermittently. If Josie Douglas returns or at the end of ninety days, Miss Brimswell and I will revisit your case again." Closing the folder in front of him with a snap, he looked over at Emma once more. "That's it for today folks. I wish they could all be this easy."

Happy and relieved, tears welled up in Emma's eyes

and she fought them back. Then she stood with Steffie in her arms as Sammy hung on to her leg.

Hannah approached her, her smile a bit wobbly. "Can I help you get them into their snowsuits?"

"Sure," she managed. "There's a sofa right outside. We can do it there."

Tucker, Jackson, Miss Brimswell and the lawyers held back as Emma and Hannah exited the room with the twins and their snowsuits.

"I know this is hard for you." Emma sat Steffie on the cushions and Hannah lowered Sammy beside her.

As she unzipped one of the snowsuits, Hannah nodded. "It is. I dreamed of being Sammy and Steffie's mother the past two months, but...there's something I want to tell you. Jackson and I are pregnant. I've known for about a month but I wanted to make sure everything was okay before I told everyone. And not only am I pregnant, but we're going to have twins!"

Enfolding Hannah into a hug, Emma said, "That's wonderful news. I'm so happy for you! I guess that does make this a little easier."

"Yes, it does, but still...is it okay if we come visit the twins? We could baby-sit."

"Of course, you can. You can visit whenever you want. I don't know how long I'm going to be at Tucker's, but even when I go back to Cedarton, you're welcome anytime."

"Thank you. That means a lot. Now let's get these two bundled up. They'll soon be yelling for lunch."

Because the twins needed their car seats, Jackson drove over to Tucker's. But then he and Hannah left, knowing that was for the best if the twins were going to get settled in. While Emma concentrated on fixing lunch for the babies, a combination of baby food and some mashed potatoes that had been left over, Tucker installed the car seats in the back seat of his truck.

By the time Tucker returned to the kitchen, Sammy had smeared mashed potatoes in his hair and Steffie had managed to dribble red beets down her bib, all over her hands and on the high chair tray.

Emma glanced up at him, and she couldn't read what he was thinking from his face. "I'll have to wash up the floor when we're through. You'll have the cleanest kitchen floor in Nebraska until I leave."

Not responding to what she'd said, he went to the refrigerator and took out packs of lunchmeat and cheese. "I guess you haven't eaten."

"I'll get something when I'm finished with them, or after I put them down for their nap."

"I can easily make three sandwiches as well as two," he offered.

"Thanks, that would be great."

"Then I'll be going into the office. Don't worry about making supper tonight, I won't be back until late."

There was something in Tucker's voice that made Emma study him carefully. It wasn't annoyance, it wasn't coolness, it was...she couldn't put her finger on it. Maybe the reality of having twins in his house was a lot different than just the idea of it. And there was something that she had to ask him.

"Tucker, do you mind if I do some baby-proofing?"

"Baby-proofing?"

"Yes. I don't want to constantly restrict Sammy and Steffie, so I'd like to rearrange your cupboards a little— put safe things like pots and pans and plastic containers down in the bottom."

He frowned. "That's fine. Do whatever you have to do to make them safe."

"I have a gate I can put at the bottom of the stairs. But I should do some shifting in the living room, too. I don't want them getting into your CDs and tapes."

"Whatever you have to do is fine, Emma." His tone was short and curt.

Steffie banged on her high chair tray then, and Sammy soon followed suit. They mimicked each other a lot, and that usually meant twice the trouble or twice the noise, but also twice the love.

"Okay, I'll get the applesauce," she told them gently, and they looked up at her with grins.

"Are you sure you have everything you need here?" Tucker asked, quickly making three sandwiches and standing at the counter to eat his.

"I think so—enough diapers, enough food, enough milk. Aunt Gertie phoned while you were outside. She said to call her if I need anything, and Hannah said the same."

After Emma dished out applesauce, she took it to the twins. Steffie reached up to her and grabbed a handful of her hair. Emma laughed, "I can see I'm going to have to take a bath when you guys do." She gave Steffie a kiss on the nose and offered her a spoonful of applesauce.

Behind her, she heard sudden movement from Tucker—the noise of the drawer opening and shutting, the tear of tinfoil against the box. Then suddenly, he was standing in the doorway. "I'm going to take the other sandwich along. I'll eat it at the office." He shoved the silver foil packet into his jacket pocket, then put on his jacket, zipped it and set his hat on his head.

"Don't you want something else with that?" Emma asked, knowing Tucker was a big eater.

"This is fine. Don't wait up for me tonight. I have a lot of paperwork to take care of."

"All right. I'll see you later then."

"Right. Later." With that, he strode down the short hall and she heard him go into the garage.

Something was bothering him, but she had the sinking feeling that he had no intention of telling her what it was.

The house was quiet when Tucker stopped in the kitchen at eleven o'clock that night. The two high chairs sat next to each other on one side of the rectangular table. Emma had moved the chair that was usually pushed in there to a corner. The counters and all surfaces were spotless—and so was the floor. Raking a hand through his hair, he went to the refrigerator for a can of soda. But when he opened the door, he saw baby bottles, jars of baby food, and several small dishes covered with plastic wrap. The soda now stood on the bottom shelf of the door.

Taking out a can of ginger ale he popped the lid, loosened his string tie and opened the top two buttons of his shirt. At the doorway to the living room he paused...his entertainment center had been rearranged. The bottom two shelves now housed toys—a can of blocks, a pull toy and two stuffed puppy dogs. He noticed the magazine rack was now empty, and the volumes were piled high on top of a set of bookshelves. A colorful quilt lay over the back of his sofa and a diaper bag was lodged next to the armchair. When he looked for the remote control, he couldn't find it, and he supposed Emma had hidden it so that Sammy and Steffie couldn't get at it.

After he decided it didn't matter—because he was tired enough to go to bed rather than watch the news—he climbed the stairs. But at the top he stopped when he heard a lovely voice singing a lullaby. The melodic, soft sound drew him toward the room. The door was open partway. Emma was sitting in the high-backed rocker, rocking slowly, singing as she watched the babies.

Tucker felt as if his heart turned upside down, and his throat tightened. He'd left so abruptly to go to work because Emma's sweet interaction with Steffie and Sammy had caused too much turmoil inside of him. He'd thought he was over Chad and Denise and once being a father. But the sight of Emma with the twins had brought all of it back...brought back longings that he'd banished.

When he took a step to leave, the floor creaked, and Emma looked up. "Hi," she said in a low voice.

He went into the room, though what he really wanted to do was go to his room and lock the door—against memories, against feelings, against yearnings he couldn't let overtake him.

"It took a while to get them to sleep," she murmured. "Lots of excitement today—a new house to explore and another new room to sleep in."

His gaze fell to the twins as hers did, and he thought he'd never seen babies look so perfectly angelic, so perfectly beautiful, just as Chad had looked in sleep. "I don't want to wake them," he mumbled and went out into the hall.

Following him, she closed the door partway, then brushed her hair away from her cheek. Tucker knew he should leave, but he'd missed seeing her the hours they'd been apart. And there was something he'd wanted to tell her that had gotten lost in the anxiety and the excitement of the past few days. "At Ben's ranch the other night..." He stopped, not exactly sure how much he wanted to say. "You were terrific with Gwen. The way you kept your cool and knew exactly what to do."

"Kept my cool! I was shaking in my shoes. But Gwen was so adamant about not going to the hospital, and once everything started to happen..." She shook her head. "When Josie was in the delivery room, I just remember the doctor saying the best thing to do was to let nature take its course. So I was hoping that was what was best to do for Gwen."

Since Emma had gotten her memory back, there had been a change in her. She was still the same sweet, caring woman, but there was a confidence about her now that hadn't been there before. Her responsibilities must have given her that. Seeing something in her hair, he ran his fingers over the strands and then smiled. "I think you're still wearing red beets."

She blushed and laughed. "I gave them their bath but I didn't get my shower. I wanted to make sure they were asleep first."

Denise used to complain about not having a minute to herself with him gone all the time, and he imagined that was doubly true with twins. Yet Emma didn't seem to resent the fact. "I'll leave my door open and listen for them while you get your shower. Just let me know when you're finished."

"That would be great, Tucker. I'm not sure how long they sleep now. Hannah said most nights they sleep straight through, but in a new place, they might awaken. I don't want them to be afraid."

"As long as they have you nearby, they won't be afraid. You're wonderful with them."

"You haven't seen me with them that often."

"I've seen you enough. I can tell." She was standing close, and he could easily put his arm around her...easily bend his head and kiss her. But since her memory had returned, circumstances were even more complicated between them. Emma wasn't a woman on her own. For the time being she was a surrogate mother.

Reining in his desire for her, he stepped away. "Just let me know when you're through. I'll be reading."

Emma nodded and gave him a smile he wished he could package up and take with him. Then she went into her room.

Taking a deep breath, he went into his.

When Emma rapped lightly on Tucker's door a half hour later, he looked up from the *Sportsman* magazine he'd been paging through in hopes of distracting himself. He'd changed into navy flannel jogging shorts. Before he'd invited Emma to stay in his house, he'd slept in the nude. Since then, he'd worn the shorts to bed. He slid his legs over the side of his king-size bed, not able to take his eyes off her. Her hair was soft and fluffy, just washed, and he swore he could smell her shampoo. Her white flannel nightgown and matching robe fell to her ankles, yet molded to her body provocatively—over her breasts…over the soft roundness of her hips. She was barefoot and looked like a vision he might have in a dream.

Her gaze fell to his chest and the curling hair that made a path down the middle of it. She was staring at it as if she was thinking about touching it. Just the thought aroused him. Standing, he approached her slowly, knowing he should send her away. But he couldn't. Something in him needed her more desperately than he could ever put into words.

As if drawn by an invisible string, she came toward him until he knew he was smelling her shampoo—a floral scent that made him think of springtime and gardens and days filled with sunshine. She was so close, and he wanted to touch her so badly.

"Emma," he warned, praying she'd turn around and leave. Yet also praying she wouldn't.

Lifting her chin, she asked simply, "What, Tucker?"

His control snapped. His good sense vanished. His determination to keep his life simple melted like ice in the sun. One of his hands slid under her hair, his other found the indentation at her waist and pulled her close. He didn't want to think, he only wanted to feel pleasure and Emma and sensations he'd long forgotten. She fit to him so perfectly, her lips to his, her softness against his hardness, her inexperience to his mastery. Though she was inexperienced, she had a deep, undulating passion that always caught him by surprise...that showed him experience meant nothing in the face of true desire.

He heard his groan, and it sounded as if it had come from his soul as he pulled her to the bed and took her down with him. He kept kissing her, drinking from her, finding that she was the key to unlocking everything that had been pent up in him for so long. When her hand sifted through his chest hair, he pushed her robe from her shoulder. She helped him peel it off. His fingers fumbled with three small buttons at the front of her gown and then they were open...and his hand was caressing creamy, soft skin that felt like heaven.

But then, suddenly, he heard a cry and then a wail, and he knew one of the twins was awake.

Emma pulled away from him, looking dazed, looking almost as if she didn't know where she was. Then her cheeks turned crimson and she sat up on the bed, turning away from him. "I don't know what came over me. I've never *done* anything like this before."

"Never?" he asked, his voice gravelly.

She was fidgeting with the buttons on her nightgown and then she reached behind her for her robe.

He handed it to her. "I shouldn't have come on to you like that."

"You didn't come on to me. I—"

The crying was louder now and filled Tucker's room.

"I have to go to Steffie. I don't want her to wake Sammy if I can help it." She still didn't look at him as she went to the door. "I know you have to get up early in the morning. I'll try to get her settled down as soon as I can. Good night, Tucker."

One moment he was gazing at the back of her white robe and the next at his closed door.

He swore loud and long. What the hell had gotten into him? He took a huge, calming breath, but his heart was still beating faster than normal, and he knew it probably would beat that way the rest of the night. All he had to do was think about those few minutes...

He was going to stay away from Emma. He was going to work long enough hours that he'd be too tired to even think about kissing her. He was going to find her sister, so Emma could go back to Cedarton and *his* life could go back to normal.

The sun was bright and shiny on Thursday morning as Emma penned the babies in the kitchen with her. They were happily playing near the bottom cupboards with pots and pans and plastic containers, throwing them, gnawing on them, fascinated by shapes and sounds. In the meantime, she sorted laundry relatively undisturbed. Emma knew she'd have to clean everything up by the end of the day before Tucker came home.

She hadn't seen Tucker much during the past week. He'd left early in the mornings and come home very late at night. She felt as if she'd made a monumental fool of herself last Friday night. She'd never been in a situation like that before—where feelings and desires had swept her onto a bed with a man. She'd never wanted to make love with anyone...before Tucker. But it'd been obvious from his absence since then, that it wasn't an experience he wanted to repeat.

When the doorbell rang, she was glad for the distraction. It wasn't as if she wasn't distracted enough by the twins. But even when she was giving her attention to them, she was thinking about Tucker.

As she opened the door and saw Cal, she grinned. He had always been such a good friend to her. She'd called him to tell him how the hearing had turned out and he'd been happy for her, assuring her he'd continue to keep watch over the farm.

Now as she motioned him inside, he was smiling.

"I'm so glad you came. I've missed you."

"How could you miss me when you didn't even know you *knew* me?"

She swatted his arm. "You know what I mean. Sammy and Steffie are in the kitchen. I made some apple muffins this morning. Could I interest you in one?"

He unzipped his red, down parka. "Actually, I not only stopped by to see how you were doing, but I wondered if you'd like to go out for lunch."

"With Sammy and Steffie?"

"Sure, with Sammy and Steffie. We'll go to the diner and liven up the place."

As she checked her watch, she realized time had gotten away from her and it was almost noon. "I could warm up their baby food before we leave and take it along. While we eat, maybe we can keep them occupied with a few French fries. But I'll need about fifteen minutes to get ready. I'd like to put on a clean blouse, maybe some makeup."

"No problem. I'll play with Sammy and Steffie. Take your time."

As Emma stood outside the gate that she'd put up at the doorway to the kitchen, she shook her head at the mess inside. A pile of clean laundry sat on the table half folded, and the rest of the kitchen looked as if a small tornado had whirled through. Actually two small tornados! But she'd have plenty of time after lunch to get it all cleaned up—before Tucker came home. That's if he even *came* home.

Cal gave her a little push toward the stairs. "Go on, the idea is to forget about all of this for a little while."

"Do you know what a good friend you are?" she asked seriously.

His grin was warm. "I have a good idea."

As Emma went upstairs, she thought about how much she liked Cal, yet he'd never caused the sensations Tucker did. He'd never made her heart race, or her hands sweat, or her limbs tremble. They'd been good friends since the day they'd met and she knew that's what they'd always be.

When Tucker pulled up in his driveway, he acknowledged that this midday trip home was unusual. But he hadn't seen Emma since Monday night, and he wanted to make sure everything was okay. He'd talked to her both Tuesday and Wednesday when he'd called from his office to tell her he wouldn't be home for supper. She'd been polite. So had he. Their civility could have caused a frost. He felt disconcerted by the way he was reacting to her and the twins…by the way he was handling all of it—or wasn't handling it.

He knew she was a capable woman, but he also knew twins were a handful. He wanted to make sure she hadn't bitten off more than she could chew. He wanted to make sure she had help if she needed it.

Leaving his gun locked in the glove compartment of his sheriff's vehicle, which is what he always did now, he went in the front door instead of through the garage. But he was surprised when he had to use his key, and even more surprised when silence met him inside. There were a few toys on the floor in the living room and no gate at the stairway. But then he saw the gate at the doorway to the kitchen...and then the condition of the kitchen. It looked as if a thief had ransacked the place. The cupboards were empty, their contents spilling onto the floor. He stepped over the gate and almost tripped on a plastic truck. Swearing, he saw the clean laundry on the table and called Emma's name.

No one answered. Stepping over the gate at the other side of the kitchen, he quickly checked the laundry room. No one there, either. But when he peered into the garage, he saw the truck was still sitting there.

Worried now, he went to the stairs and called up. When no one answered, he took them in a hurry and searched the bedrooms. But there was no sign of Emma or the twins.

Telling himself not to panic, he picked up the phone and called Gertie at the day-care center. But after a few moments it was clear she hadn't seen or talked to Emma. More than worried now, Tucker called Gwen Crowe and then Dana McCormack. But neither of them had seen or heard from Emma. With panic kicking in, Tucker told himself to stay calm. But one overriding question made him reach for the phone once more. What if Emma had lost her memory again? What if she didn't know who she was or where she was? What if she was wandering around somewhere with the babies...?

He was the sheriff of Cedar County, and he had the department at his disposal. One way or another, he was going to find Emma, and he was going to find her soon.

Chapter Six

Tucker was cruising the streets of Storkville, looking for a copper-haired woman carrying twins, when the call came in for him about a half-hour later. One of the deputies had spotted her at Vern's Diner.

Vern's Diner? What was she doing there? With the babies?

Covering the few short blocks to the diner in record speed, he parked much too near to the corner in front, then hurried inside. Deputy Ed Barnes was waiting for him, motioning toward the back corner. "She's back there. I came in for a cup of coffee and spotted her."

Tucker's gaze swept to the corner and there Emma was at a table with the twins on booster seats with…Cal Swenson. What the *hell* was she doing with him?

When he swore, Ed looked at him speculatively. "Do you want me to stay?"

Tucker felt like an absolute idiot. He'd practically put an APB out on Emma and here she was on a lunch date. "No, you can go," Tucker snapped.

The middle-aged deputy, with his thinning brown hair and potbelly, had a twinkle in his brown eyes. "I guess I'll tell the guys you found her."

"Yeah," Tucker muttered, "you do that." Then he strode toward the table in the corner, not sure what he was going to say.

As he approached the foursome, a burst of laughter came from first Emma, then Cal. Steffie had taken a French fry dipped in ketchup and smeared it across her face. She looked as if she had a red mustache. Tenderly, Emma leaned close to the baby and dabbed the ketchup away with her napkin. On the other side of Sammy, Cal looked on fondly—too fondly, Tucker thought.

When he'd gotten close enough to the table to hover over her, Emma looked up at him, surprised. "Tucker, what are *you* doing here?"

"More to the point," he said, "what are *you* doing here? I stopped at home. The place looked as if it had been ransacked and there wasn't hide nor hair of you or the babies."

Cal straightened in his chair. "I thought she could use an outing. Besides, we had some catching up to do." The blond man was defensive and protective of Emma, and that made Tucker even more annoyed.

"I thought you'd lost your memory again. I thought maybe you'd wandered off," he blurted out.

Looking embarrassed, Emma apologized. "I'm sorry, Tucker. I never thought you'd be home in the middle of the day. I didn't even expect you—"

No, she wouldn't have expected him. He'd been avoiding her like the plague, and he had no right to be here scolding her like a jealous suitor. Since Emma had come into his life, he wasn't sure he even knew himself anymore.

"Did you come home because you had news about Josie?" she asked hopefully.

"No. No news yet. That probably means she's not in a hurry to be found."

Disappointment showed on Emma's face. "Why *did* you come home then?"

"Just to check up on you—make sure everything was going okay," he added grudgingly.

Cal's brows arched. "As you can see, she's just fine. We're having a great time, and I'll make sure I get her home safe and sound."

Frowning at Cal's tone, which was almost adversarial, Emma asked Tucker, "Would you like to join us? We could pull over another chair."

No way. In this case, five was definitely a crowd. "No thanks. I've wasted enough time on a wild-goose chase. Next time, Emma, leave a note."

She met his gaze squarely. "I would have left a note this time if I had thought it mattered."

Tucker felt his cheeks flush. Okay, he deserved that one. He'd better set the record straight right now, in front of Cal Swenson. "It matters, Emma—*you* matter." Though he wished damned well she didn't. "I've got to get back. I'll see you tonight."

"Will you?" she asked, her chin raised, obviously thinking about the past two nights when she hadn't seen him at all.

"Yes. I'll be home for supper."

Her heart beating rapidly, Emma watched Tucker walk away without a goodbye and wondered just what all that had meant.

Cal gave Sammy another French fry from his plate. "So...what's going on between you and the sheriff?"

Blushing, Emma picked up the last quarter of her club

sandwich. *She* wasn't even sure. So what could she tell Cal? "He feels...responsible for me. He's been sort of looking out for me ever since the night I was mugged."

"He's looking out for you all right," Cal muttered. "It looked to me as if he didn't like the idea of you having lunch with me."

"I don't think it had anything to do with you. I think he was just worried."

"Emma, girl, I think it had *everything* to do with me. He sees me as a rival."

"That's ridiculous. I told him we're friends."

"That doesn't mean he believed you. Besides, he might think I want to be more than friends—even if that's not true for you."

"We are just friends, aren't we, Cal?"

"When I first met you, I think I wanted more than that. But then I realized I was the kind of guy who never liked to stay at home. And you were the kind of woman who *loved* being at home."

She'd realized that same thing, and she imagined that's why their friendship had evolved into something strong and easy, rather than romantic. "I value your friendship, Cal."

He grinned. "And I value yours. But mark my words, Emma. Tucker Malone wants more than friendship from you."

If he did, he had a good way of hiding it. She knew she wanted more than friendship from Tucker, but that could be a lost cause. With a sigh, she tried to push thoughts of the sexy sheriff aside. "How about sharing a banana split?"

Wagging his finger at her, he scolded, "You're changing the subject. But I'll let you do it. A banana split it is."

* * *

Somehow Emma managed to put supper on the table by the time the twins were clamoring for their meal. Tucker walked in while Sammy banged on his tray.

"Go ahead and get started, I'll catch bites in between feeding them," she said.

Tucker hung up his hat and jacket. "I'll be down in five minutes. I'm going to get comfortable."

As good as his words, Tucker was back a few minutes later, dressed in a black T-shirt and jogging pants. Her gaze dipped to the string at his waist, but then she quickly looked away and gave Sammy another spoonful of carrots.

Taking in the scene at a glance, Tucker pulled his chair close to Steffie's. "Your food will get cold if you try to feed both of them."

To Emma's amazement, Tucker picked up Steffie's divided dish, took the small spoon in his hand and started feeding her like a pro. He'd done this before, Emma could tell. He looked too comfortable with the whole procedure.

Finally the twins seemed satisfied and as they finger fed themselves pieces of zwieback cookies that Emma had broken apart, Tucker and Emma finished their meals. They ate in silence until Emma said, "I'm sorry you were worried about me today."

"I shouldn't have assumed the worst. I never expected you'd be going out with Cal."

"It wasn't a date, Tucker."

"Wasn't it?"

"No!"

Avoiding her gaze, he laid down his fork. "You're the same age, you come from the same town, you've known each other a long time. You looked as if you were having a good time. He likes the twins—"

"As I've told you once before, Tucker, we're friends."

Tucker picked up his mug of coffee and took a sip, then eyed her over the rim. "Have you dated much?"

Her cheeks flushed. "No, I haven't. I haven't had time. I've either been working, or taking care of Josie, or taking care of the twins."

"You deserve to have some fun, Emma...to have a life of your own."

She shrugged. "I *do* have a life of my own. It's full of lots of love and caring. No, I haven't gone out on many dates, but the truth is, I don't want to date just to have a good time. I want to be with somebody I like and care about...who sees possibilities in a relationship beyond a night in bed."

As if he was uneasy, he shifted on his chair. "About that night in my room—"

She waited.

"I didn't mean to take advantage of you."

"You didn't take advantage of me. I knew exactly what I was doing."

Looking startled, he put down his coffee mug. "And what *were* you doing?"

"I was doing what you were doing. We were exploring some kind of chemistry that's been between us since the night we met."

"That's one way of putting it." He pinned her with a hard stare. "But you just said you wanted more than just one night in bed. Don't look for that from me, Emma. I've told you before—I'm not husband or father material." Pushing back his chair, he stood. "I'll be working in my den if you need anything."

Then he removed himself from Emma and the twins quickly—as if he had to prove he wasn't a family man.

As if he had to prove something to himself, as much as to her.

Tucker worked in his den, finally leaning back in his swivel chair after an hour and rolling his shoulders. He'd posted information about Josie Douglas on several law enforcement message boards, hoping to get a new lead somewhere—anywhere. There was one thing he hadn't covered with Emma, and he might as well take care of it now.

When he'd entered his den, he'd closed the door and tried to forget the feelings that had barraged him as he'd fed Steffie and wiped food from her mouth with a napkin. Yes, he'd been away from home a lot when he was married, but when he *was* there, he'd helped with Chad as often as he could. He'd given Denise breaks so she could go shopping or simply have lunch with friends. Maybe what they hadn't done was take enough time for the two of them. Nights in bed weren't the same as companionable hours spent together—building friendship—as well as learning how to give each other pleasure. He'd made every mistake in the book with Denise.

When he opened the den's door, he didn't hear sounds in the living room. But halfway up the steps he could hear giggling and laughter from the bathroom. From the doorway, he could see Emma kneeling beside the sunken tub, trying to bathe Sammy and Steffie, who were sitting in bath seats.

He stepped inside, seeing Sammy and Steffie splash, and splash a lot. Emma had the sleeves of her oxford blouse rolled up but there were water spots all over it, delineating the outline of her bra.

Tucker would have backed out again, except she

looked up at him and smiled. "This would be a lot easier if I got in with them!"

He couldn't help but smile. "Do you need another hand?"

If she was surprised, she didn't show it. "I sure could. Two slippery babies are a little more than one person can handle."

Yet she had handled them perfectly well the past few days. Still, he'd offered to give her help if she needed it. Picking up one of the two green bath towels she'd laid on the sink, he took it to the tub, laid it down on the edge, then lifted Sammy out onto it, wrapping the little boy with it. Then he grabbed a hand towel and made a game of rubbing down Sammy's hair. The little boy squealed and giggled and wriggled until Tucker caught him in his arms, towel and all, holding him against his chest.

Emma did the same thing with Steffie. "Their hair's so fine, it dries before I even get them to bed."

"What's their ritual?" he asked, knowing every kid had one.

"First I close the door so neither of them can escape."

He gave her a wry grin as Sammy nestled against his shoulder.

"And then we sit on a quilt on the floor and play with blocks for a little while. I rock one, then the other, and eventually kiss them good-night. It's not very complicated."

Tucker stood with Sammy in his arms. "I'll help get this guy dressed. I think he might be asleep before you even think about building something with blocks."

"They missed their nap this afternoon. After Cal brought us back, he played with them for awhile."

When Tucker thought about that—about Cal Swenson

playing with Steffie and Sammy—he was definitely disconcerted. He remembered again feeding Steffie her supper and now realized how much he enjoyed having Sammy in his arms. Before memories of what he'd lost got the better of him, he took Sammy to the nursery, picked up the sleeper on the changing table, and easily slipped the baby into it.

When Emma set Steffie on the quilt on the floor, he said, "I came up to ask you for a list of Josie's friends. That's one avenue we haven't explored."

After thinking about it a few moments, Emma replied, "I don't know what to tell you. She lost contact with school friends, and for the past year, both of us have been busy with the twins."

"You don't have any kind of list?"

Emma shook her head. "It's only now I realize how isolated we were. Maybe that's what drove Josie away as much as anything else. I should have encouraged her to join some clubs, do activities with kids her own age."

"She's the one who got herself pregnant, Emma."

Emma's gaze met his. "I know."

When Tucker brought Sammy over to the quilt, he knelt down beside Emma. They were both on their knees, very close to each other. The hum between them hadn't desisted just because he'd decided it should. His gaze went to her breasts under her wet blouse, then returned to her face.

But this time Emma was the one who backed up, her cheeks rosier then they'd been before. She turned away from him and ran her fingers gently through Steffie's hair. "Thanks for helping me, Tucker."

Apparently, she'd taken his little speech awhile ago to heart. Rising to his feet, he convinced himself that was a good thing.

When he would have left the room, she stopped him. "It's hard to believe Thursday's Thanksgiving already. Aunt Gertie asked me if we want to join her and her family for dinner. Do you want to?"

Every year since he'd been in Storkville, Gertie had asked him to join her. But he'd always refused. Holidays had been something to avoid or get through, not enjoy. But as he cast a glance at Emma and thought about the twins, he conceded that this year might be different. "I think I would. What about you?"

"I'd like to go, too. I've never spent Thanksgiving with a lot of people. It's usually just me and Josie and the twins, plus Cal when he's around. But he told me he has plans this year."

"Then tell Gertie she'll have a few more guests."

"There was something else I wanted to ask you," Emma said.

He gazed down at her, studying her carefully.

"Do you mind if I have a belated birthday party for the twins? I hate to let their first year go by without celebrating it."

He remembered from their birth certificates that they had been a year old on October 29th. "When would you like to have it?"

"Well, Jackson and Hannah are going out of town this weekend. I know they'd like to come. Weekdays wouldn't be good for Gwen and Ben because of Nathan and school. I'd like everybody to be here! What about the day after Thanksgiving? I thought I'd also ask Aunt Gertie, Dana and Quentin McCormack and Penny Sue. And, of course, Cal."

Of course, Cal. "Do you think we have enough room here?" Tucker asked brusquely.

"Oh, sure. It probably won't last long. We'll just have

snacks—ice cream, cake, potato chips. I think it'll be fun.''

It had been a long time since Tucker had had fun in his life. When he thought about decorating with balloons, as well as buying the twins' presents, he liked the idea more and more. ''Okay, the Friday after Thanksgiving it is. Just give me a list of everything you want and I'll take care of it.''

''No, *I'll* take care of it. They're my niece and nephew, and I have a checkbook now.''

He could see she was going to be stubborn about this. ''Tell you what. You take care of the food, and I'll take care of the decorations and incidentals. How's that?''

She gave him a wary look. ''Are you going to define 'incidentals'?''

''Nope. But they're nonnegotiable. Every party needs incidentals.''

She laughed, then gave in. ''All right.''

Tucker looked down at the twins once more. ''Good night, Steffie. Good night, Sammy.'' Then he gazed at Emma. ''I'll see you in the morning.''

After she nodded, he left the room. Out in the hall, he realized how good he felt. Better than he'd felt in a long time. Whether he liked it or not, Emma was changing his life. He might as well enjoy it.

On the day after Thanksgiving at the sheriff's office, Tucker received the call he'd been waiting for. The butler at the McCormack estate was back in town. Wasting no time, Tucker made an appointment with Mr. Harriman for a half hour later, hoping this was the break he needed. He had mixed feelings about searching for the twins' father. Yet their father might know where Josie was. Above all else, he wanted to find Emma's sister for her.

Tucker spent over an hour with the butler and ended up with more questions than answers. After a stop at Chez Stork, where he interviewed the maître d' and a waitress, he called Jackson Caldwell's office. But Jackson had a full roster of patients to see, and Tucker told him he'd talk to him tonight. Taking a quick detour to the General Store, Tucker filled the back of his sheriff's vehicle with helium balloons, then headed back to his office. He'd purchased an assortment of toys for Sammy and Steffie earlier in the week, along with paper plates, napkins and cups, which he'd given to Emma, telling her they'd make cleanup easier.

Eating a sandwich at his desk a short time later, Tucker thought again about dinner yesterday at Gertie's. Thanksgiving had been...unsettling. The dinner had been more than satisfying, the games of charades afterward, relaxing and fun. But he'd been in turmoil most of the evening, feeling part of a large family, yet knowing he *wasn't* part of it. He'd told Emma he wasn't a family man—and he wasn't. He'd royally screwed up his attempt at it.

His phone rang, a welcome intrusion to his thoughts, and Tucker got another break in the Josie Douglas case. She'd received a ticket yesterday in Kearney, Nebraska, for parking in a no-parking zone. Kearney was about four hours away. Finally, a solid lead. He'd placed her at last. The problem was, he didn't know if she was staying in Kearney or just driving through. Instead of getting Emma's hopes up, he'd wait to tell her about the ticket until he'd alerted the police there and checked motels in the area.

That night everyone arrived at Tucker's house by seven o'clock to celebrate the twins' birthday. Dana and Quentin brought Dana's three-year-old triplets, though it was obvious they considered Quentin their dad now since his marriage to Dana in October. Gwen's new baby, Nathan, and the five little ones kept all of the adults busy—laughing, serving and cleaning up spilled juice and gobs of icing that somehow managed to make it to the floor.

Emma and Tucker helped the twins open present after present as everyone chatted and continued to eat. Emma sat on the sofa next to Tucker, her shoulder companionably brushing his as Sammy held on to a terry cloth giraffe Tucker had gotten him and Steffie chewed on a colorful rattle. In addition to those, Tucker had bought them both rocking horses—one in blue and one in pink—for when they were a little older.

Emma leaned close to him so he could hear her above all the voices. "Thank you for making tonight special."

"I didn't do anything," he murmured.

"Yes, you did. Besides helping me get this organized, you put a lot of effort into the toys you picked out and the decorations. I'm glad Hannah and Dana have their cameras so we have plenty of pictures."

"What you need is a video camera," he observed.

She laughed. "Not in the budget this year!"

Maybe he'd buy a video camera for himself and convince Emma it was something he'd always wanted. That way he could make tapes and she'd have them forever. He wished now he'd had videotapes of Chad. If he could see him again, hear his voice...

Tucker pushed the idea away and went to the kitchen for another piece of cake.

By the coffee pot, Jackson asked, "What did you want to see me about?"

Tucker decided now was as good a time as any to ask him a few questions. "I found out some interesting information today."

"About?"

There was no way to beat around the bush. "Mr. Harriman told me that Josie Douglas worked parties on the McCormack Estate, and she also filled in temporarily for maids."

"Did Quentin know her?" Jackson asked.

"Until his recent marriage, he'd spent long hours at his office. So he'd never seen her there."

"I see."

Tucker took out a picture of Josie he had in his shirt pocket. "You're sure you've never seen her before?"

Jackson studied the picture again. "Nope, never have. I told you that."

"I know. But I learned something else from Harriman."

Jackson looked puzzled. "What?"

"He said that Josie Douglas and your father were pretty chummy."

Jackson looked wary. "Define 'pretty chummy'."

"On more than one occasion at parties at the estate, he found them embracing or kissing in a secluded corner."

"You've *got* to be kidding."

"I'm not kidding, Jackson. I think it's quite possible that your father was also Sammy and Steffie's father."

"Jackson Caldwell, Sr. is...*was*...Sammy and Steffie's father?" Emma asked in astonishment from the doorway. "How long have you known this?"

"I don't know for certain. But I began putting the pieces together today," Tucker answered her, wishing he'd spoken with Jackson outside.

"Why didn't you tell me?" Her voice was accusing, as if he'd deliberately kept it from her.

"I wanted to talk to Jackson first."

Recovering from his stunned silence, Jackson said, "I

can't help you. I don't know anything about it. But if what you say is true, then Sammy and Steffie—''

''Are your half brother and sister,'' Tucker filled in. ''We're not going to know for certain, of course, until I find Josie. But the maître d' and waitress at Chez Stork saw them together a few times in the restaurant's private back room. I also checked out the motel on the edge of town. The owner there recognized them. He remembered seeing them there twice. Your father paid him handsomely to forget that they'd registered. But since your father died, the man no longer feels obligated to keep his silence. He checked his records for me, and their one rendezvous took place nine months, almost to the day, before Sammy and Steffie were born.''

''I can't believe this,'' Emma said. ''Josie and Jackson Caldwell, Sr.? What could he see in someone so young?''

Tucker cleared his throat. He knew the elder Caldwell's reputation, but he didn't want Emma to know. ''Older men sometimes see themselves as…well… protectors of younger women.'' He might as well give Caldwell the benefit of the doubt.

''Protectors?'' Emma raised her brows. ''Tell me something, Tucker. Is there anything *else* you've found out about Josie that you haven't told me?''

Uncomfortable with keeping information from her, he raked his hand through his hair and decided she might as well know. ''Josie was ticketed in Kearney yesterday for parking in a no-parking zone.''

''Why didn't you tell me? This is our first real trace of her!''

This is exactly what he'd been trying to prevent… raising false hopes. ''But it isn't, Emma. That's the point. I don't have anything else. I'm checking with the police department there, and motels in the area. You had enough on your mind with the party tonight.''

"Listen to me, Tucker. You might be older than I am, but that doesn't mean you know better. It doesn't mean I need your protection. If you find out something about my sister, I want to know about it.''

Jackson was looking at the two of them curiously.

"This is an ongoing investigation,'' Tucker tossed back, using his law enforcement voice. ''And although you're an interested party, Emma, *I'm* the one who decides what information I tell you and what information I don't.''

Where before she looked angry, now she looked upset. ''I see. So...although you feel the need to protect me, I'm just another citizen of Storkville who'll be informed when you deem it necessary. I thought we were further than that, Tucker. I thought we'd built up some level of trust.''

The awkward silence in the kitchen was only relieved by the ticking of the clock over the sink. It was broken when Gertie appeared in the doorway, cuddling Steffie in her arms. ''This one's ready for bed, and some of your guests are ready to leave.'' She eyed all of them as if she knew she'd barged in on something private, as if maybe she'd even done it on purpose.

Taking Steffie from Aunt Gertie's arms, Emma cuddled the little girl on her shoulder. ''I'll take her upstairs.''

"Hannah has Sammy,'' Gertie added. ''I'm sure she'd like to help you put them to bed.''

Emma nodded.

Tucker didn't want Emma to leave the kitchen like this. He didn't want her to think he considered her just another citizen of Storkville. But what *did* he consider her?

He had to find the answer to that question, and find it soon, or he'd be in deeper trouble than Josie Douglas.

Chapter Seven

When Sammy and Steffie awakened on Saturday morning, Emma was dressing. She hadn't slept much, thinking about her argument of sorts with Tucker last night. She'd overreacted. She never should have made that comment about him being older. It seemed to be a touchy subject with him, and she'd made a point of using it to her advantage. It was just…

He'd almost made it sound as if she were a stranger staying in his house. That had hurt because he had become so much more to her…more than she wanted to admit. They'd have to talk. Maybe after she got the twins some breakfast.

But as she hurried into Sammy and Steffie's room, she saw the door to Tucker's bedroom was open. When she dressed the twins, she heard no sounds coming from downstairs.

After she took the children to the first floor and put the gates up to keep them in the kitchen, she saw the note lying on the table. Picking it up she read:

Emma,
I'll be working at the Thrift Shop on Main Street today. The deputies' wives want to open it before Christmas, and they need help painting. I should be home by late afternoon.

Tucker

Emma had heard about the Thrift Shop project. There had been an article in the newspaper. The deputies' wives had brought it to life, filling another need in Storkville for residents who needed good clothes at affordable prices, especially children's clothing. But Emma was disappointed she wouldn't be seeing Tucker all day.

She'd also been hoping Tucker could watch the twins for a few hours so she could get some much-needed work done. She'd used some of her savings to catch up on bills from the last two months, but now she needed to start a stream of income again. Fortunately, monthly checks came in for Web sites she kept updated. But she had contracts for ten new Web sites to design, and she wouldn't receive the money for them until they were finished and up-and-running.

Thank goodness her clients had been understanding when she'd explained briefly why she'd been delayed for the past two months. But now she didn't want to give them an excuse to find someone else to do the work. Maybe Aunt Gertie could watch the twins for a few hours if she was free.

Aunt Gertie was delighted when Emma called her. She came right over and parked her motorized shopping cart on the front lawn. Then she shooed Emma into Tucker's den and told her not to worry about a thing. She and the twins would have a wonderful time together.

Emma trusted Aunt Gertie as much as she did Tucker

and worked steadily for the next three hours, pleased with what she accomplished. But in the back of her mind, she was still disconcerted by her argument with Tucker and she made a quick decision.

Fifteen minutes later, she drove to the Thrift Shop in Tucker's truck, a can of cookies on the seat beside her. She'd made a double batch for the party last night and these had been left over. She was sure everyone at the Thrift Shop would enjoy them, and the snack might give her a chance to mend fences with Tucker.

When she pulled open the heavy glass door and went inside the empty store, she found a bustle of activity and the smell of fresh paint. She recognized Earl Grimes' wife, Betty, and Barry Sanchek's wife, Camille. Both women brought their children to the day-care center. While they were putting together a stand of shelves, Tucker was picking up a drop cloth from the corner of the room.

After Emma said hello to the women, she headed in his direction. He was wearing worn jeans with a few rips and tears and a faded blue T-shirt that was now paint-splattered. He looked as handsomely rugged as he always did, and Emma's heart raced faster.

He didn't smile when he saw her coming.

"Hi," she said quickly, not knowing where to start. "Aunt Gertie's watching the twins." She offered him the can. "I thought you might like a snack."

"We were about ready to take a lunch break. I'll put these over by the coffee urn so everybody can enjoy them." He took the can and would have crossed to the other side of the room, but she clasped his arm, needing to clear the air.

He looked down at her hand, as if he didn't want it there. But something told her she had to keep hold of him. "I'm sorry I overreacted last night. Sometimes I can't tell what's personal between us, and what's part of your investigation."

The tension in his body seemed to dissipate somewhat, and he set the can on the ladder. "The lines get crossed," he agreed but didn't go any further.

"Tucker, what I said about you being older…I was upset. It wasn't meant as a criticism."

"I was never touchy about my age until you dropped into Storkville," he muttered.

"Why did my coming to Storkville make a difference?"

His gaze remained steady on hers. He seemed to debate with himself for a moment, but finally admitted, "Because the thoughts I have about you are inappropriate. You're young, innocent…"

Frustrated with him, she cut him off and, though her voice went low, it was vehement. "I'm twenty-five years old, Tucker, and old enough to know who I am and what I'm doing. I've been on my own for a long time. I might have *wanted* to be a princess in an high tower, but I never was. I had to face reality early and I still am. So don't you use that as an excuse for not wanting to get close to me. I think thirty-seven is the *perfect* age for a man to—" She stopped abruptly.

A glimmer of a smile twinkled in his eyes. "To what?"

"To do whatever he wants to do," she finished in a burst of embarrassment that reddened her cheeks.

Raking his hand through his hair, he shook his head. "You never cease to amaze me."

"I'll consider that a good thing," she responded with a bit of a snap.

He laughed out loud. "You're right. It probably is. Life was getting a bit boring until you came to town."

She smiled at him then and was about to tell him what he had done for *her* life, when Camille Sanchek crossed to them. "Betty and I were just talking and we wondered if you'd be interested with helping getting the Thrift Shop set up?"

"Sure," Emma responded. "I'd love to help."

But Tucker intervened. "Emma, with the twins, don't you think you have enough to handle?"

He was being protective again, but she loved that about him. All of a sudden, like a strike of lightning, she realized—she *loved* Tucker Malone.

"Emma?" Camille asked.

She tried to clear her head. "I'm sorry. I didn't hear what you said."

"I asked if it would be too much work. You don't have to come down *here* to help."

Taking a deep breath, trying to absorb the overwhelming realization of her feelings for Tucker, she answered, "I'd like to help. The people of this town have been so good to me and the twins. What can I do?"

"We need someone to sort the clothes before we bring them here."

"Oh, that's easy. I can do that while the twins are playing. Sure, just drop them off."

"Is that all right with you, Tucker?" Camille asked.

"Sure. There's plenty of room in the garage before and after Emma sorts them."

"I really appreciate this. If we can get this store open before Christmas, we'll make everyone's holidays a little happier." She would have walked away then, but she turned back to them. "We have a yearly ritual. Everyone we know who puts up a tree comes and tags one at our

farm the Sunday after Thanksgiving. We have hot chocolate, cookies and wagon rides. Do you want to come
join us?''

Emma looked up at Tucker. ''Do you put up a tree?''

''Not usually. But this year could be an exception with
the twins there. Would you like to go?''

She nodded.

Camille smiled and moved away. ''We'll expect you
then. It should be lots of fun.''

''I'll have to find someone to watch Sammy and Steffie,'' Emma said.

''I'll bet Hannah would love to.''

Emma suddenly felt closer to Tucker at this moment
than she'd ever felt. It would be good for them to spend
some time alone together tomorrow. Maybe then she
could learn what *he* felt for *her*.

Winter had come to Storkville early this year. The
crisp, clear cold was relieved slightly by the sun peeking
through clouds. Tucker and Emma had taken a wagon
ride to a field with a multitude of Scotch pines and tagged
one they liked. As they rode back to the barn in a wagon
full of people, the arm of Emma's coat jostled against
Tucker's flannel shirtsleeve. He'd only worn a heavy
shirt and his insulated vest, but he didn't need a coat to
keep him warm when he was hip-to-hip and arm-to-arm
beside Emma on a hay bale.

''Are you cold?'' Tucker asked her, hoping the frosty
weather would keep his desire in check as he tried to
concentrate on the scenery.

''I'm fine,'' she answered him. ''At least until we get
to the bonfire.''

He laughed. Barry had started a bonfire for the more
hearty souls who liked the outdoors.

When they stopped in back of the barn, Tucker helped Emma from the wagon and they walked to the bonfire at the edge of the partially frozen pond. Other families scurried onto the wagon to take their ride to the field. Those who'd returned with Tucker and Emma went into the house. The nearby pine trees softly whistled with the wind as Tucker and Emma stood watching the fire.

He supposed he should tell her about next Friday night. "My monthly poker game is at my house next week on Friday night. I thought I should mention it. I'll tell the guys they can't smoke because of the twins."

She looked surprised he'd thought of that. "Will that be a hardship?" she asked teasingly.

"Maybe. But I'll get extra food so they don't notice it."

She laughed. "I can make snacks that'll be better than potato chips."

"You don't have to do that."

"I want to, Tucker."

Emma was the most giving woman he'd ever met. The fire in front of them, the grove of trees to the side of them, voices in the distance, gave them privacy he was well aware of. He couldn't believe how much he wanted Emma, even out here. To push his thoughts onto another track, he said, "If you want to work tonight, I can watch Sammy and Steffie."

"That would be a big help. I got a lot done yesterday with Aunt Gertie there, but I have two sites I'd like to finish up."

"Did you go to school to learn what you do?"

"No, I'm self-taught. When I graduated from high school, I took a job selling computers at a local store. There were lots of free perks. The owner let me try out one of the new computers at home, and I could take home any manual I wanted. So I educated myself. I found I really liked designing Web sites. As the years passed, there became more of a need for it, and soon I had a client list at the store. A few years ago I decided to make it a home business.''

They stared into the fire for what seemed like a long time. Then Tucker couldn't help but ask, ''What are you thinking about?''

Her answer was immediate. ''You…me. I don't understand why you think we're so different when we get along so well.''

Her honesty took him aback. ''It has to do with experience as much as years, I guess. As an undercover cop, I saw a side of life you'll never want to see. It's probably not even within the grasp of your imagination— and that's a good thing. It changed me, Emma.'' He paused for a moment, then went on, ''You don't want to believe it, but you *are* innocent. You haven't been exposed to the baser side of life or the baser side of men.''

Facing him rather than the fire, she asked, ''Did you ever think that maybe I'm tired of being innocent?''

Her eyes were so huge and sparkling with emotions that pulled him closer to her. Settling his hands on her shoulders he murmured, ''Oh, Emma. You'd run in the other direction if you ever saw *my* baser side.''

She reached up and lightly touched his jaw. ''I could never be scared of you.''

Her complete trust was his undoing. He didn't deserve it. He didn't deserve anything about her. But he wanted her trust, and he wanted her. With a fierceness that could make him shake if he'd let it, drawing her into his arms, he hungrily took her lips, wanting to see if she *did* trust him…or if the extent of his desire was too much for her to handle. Yet she fervently responded, stroking his tongue with hers, weaving her hands into his hair, holding onto him as if she never wanted to let him go.

Even the cold couldn't keep his desire in check. Their passion burned it away until he lifted his head and gazed down at her. His voice was husky as he asked, "Are you ready to go inside?"

She just nodded.

The afternoon seemed to speed by as Emma talked with the deputies and their wives, as well as other friends of the Sancheks. But all the while, her gaze didn't stray from Tucker. She drank hot chocolate and wished he'd kiss her again. At least this time when he'd kissed her, he hadn't told her it was a mistake. At least today, he hadn't retreated into himself as he so often did.

When they finally returned to Tucker's house, it was around four o'clock. Jackson and Hannah were sitting on the floor in the living room with the twins. Jackson was tickling Sammy and making him giggle. After Emma joined them on the floor and Tucker took a seat on the sofa, Hannah asked, "Did you have fun?"

"It was great," Emma responded. But as she watched Jackson with Sammy, she wondered what would happen if Jackson Caldwell Sr. *had* been the twins' father.

As if Jackson was reading her mind, he said, "Emma, Hannah and I know you've been through a lot. We don't want you to worry about us taking the twins away from you. Even if my father fathered them, we know they belong with you. We'd just like to stay close."

"Absolutely, you can. Oh, Jackson, thank you for saying that. I was so worried."

"Hannah figured you would be." As Sammy crawled to a ball across the room, Jackson stood. "We'd better be getting home. We enjoyed this afternoon, and it gave us more opportunity to practice. So whenever you need baby-sitters give us a call.''

Tucker kept watch over the twins while Emma saw Hannah and Jackson out. When she returned to the living room, she noticed Sammy pulling himself up by the armchair. Then he looked over at Tucker.

Tucker smiled at the little boy and beckoned to him. ''Come on, Sammy, you can do it. Give it a try.''

For the past few weeks, Sammy had been making his way from one piece of furniture to the next, walking, yet not truly walking on his own. Now he looked over at Tucker, and then with a happy little sound took off toward him. One, two, three steps and he was in Tucker's arms. Tears came to Emma's eyes. When she looked at Tucker again, she expected him to be smiling, but there was such a pained expression on his face.

She went over to the sofa and sat down beside him. After she praised Sammy for his feat, she nonchalantly said to Tucker, ''You've never told me if you were ever married.''

Sammy wriggled in Tucker's arms, and Tucker set him down on the floor where he promptly sank to his knees and crawled off toward his sister.

''I was married once. But it didn't work out.''

''When you were a cop in Chicago?''

He nodded.

''Was it because of your police work that it didn't work out?'' she probed.

''That and other things.''

''And you don't want to talk about it.''

''I don't want to talk about it.''

Maybe he hadn't retreated from her after their kiss, but he was retreating again now. She was sure it had something to do with his marriage. When would he trust her enough to tell her?

As an undercover cop, Tucker had learned how to compartmentalize—separate one part of his life from another. But this morning as he sat in his office at the sheriff's department working, he was doing a hellish poor job of it. He kept remembering yesterday's kiss with Emma at the bonfire. On top of that, he could hear Sammy's glee as he'd taken his first few steps.

Focusing on the reports on his desk, he compared Barry Sanchek's interview of Gertie Anderson after Emma's mugging with Earl Grimes' interview of the teacher from the high school. There'd been an update on the report of the latest mugging since the last time he'd read it. The victim stated she'd gotten a glimpse of a short ponytail sticking out the back of the nylon stocking.

With attention to the most minute detail, Tucker went over Gertie's interview again. He hadn't paid much attention to it before, but tucked in amongst the quotes and notes, Tucker noticed that Gertie had described the mugger's belt buckle. It had been a deer head cast in silver. Leaning back in his chair, Tucker envisioned it. He'd seen one of those recently. But he couldn't put his finger on exactly *where* he'd seen it.

Then suddenly, he remembered. A ponytail and that belt buckle. Enough for a warrant. If he was lucky, he'd have Emma's mugger in custody before sundown.

After Emma put the twins to bed, she went downstairs and stared at the phone in the living room. She was worried and not sure what to do. Tucker hadn't come home for supper and hadn't called. What would he think if she called him at his office?

Not caring *what* he thought at this point, deciding to give him a piece of her mind, she went to the kitchen. If he got angry with her, she'd deal with it.

As she opened the drawer for the phone book, she thought about how quiet he'd become last night after he'd told her that he'd been married. Tucker had to learn that silence wasn't always golden. Maybe she was the one who could teach him that.

She'd no sooner picked up the phone, than she heard a car pull into the driveway. But the garage door didn't go up. Going into the living room, she looked out the window and saw Tucker coming up the walk with Barry Sanchek beside him. Tucker's arm was in a sling!

When the door opened, Emma was there waiting.

Tucker was pale. Barry was holding a drugstore bag in his hand and looked concerned.

"What happened?" she asked.

"We caught your mugger," Tucker said in a low voice as he went into the living room and sank down into the armchair very carefully.

She looked at Barry for more of an explanation because she had a feeling Tucker wasn't going to give it to her.

"As the sheriff said, he caught your mugger. After he put two and two together from the reports, he realized the man we'd driven home from the Red Ball last week had worn a belt buckle like Gertie Anderson described after your mugging—*and* had a ponytail like our last victim described. The judge issued a warrant, and we found your pocketbook in his house, along with his latest victim's wallet. Of course he wasn't there. His wife told us he was at the Red Ball again, so Tucker headed on over while we searched the house more thoroughly."

"Tucker went alone? Without backup?"

"He's the sheriff, Miss Douglas. He can do pretty much what he wants. It turns out our suspect didn't like the idea of being read his Miranda rights, and Tucker had to take him down. But not before the man threw a chair at Tucker and it hit his shoulder."

Unable to stay away from him any longer, she went over to the side of the chair and knelt down. "Are you all right?"

"Don't make a fuss, Emma. I'll be fine tomorrow."

Emma looked over his shoulder at Barry. "Will he?"

"According to the doc at the hospital, he's going to be sore for a few days, and he's not supposed to drive."

"Like hell, I'm not driving," Tucker muttered.

Barry held up the bag. "If he wants to suffer in silence without the pain medication, the doc said that was okay. But he should take the other stuff he gave him. It will help the swelling and inflammation."

"I'll see to it that he takes it," she assured Barry.

At that Tucker gave her a dark look, swiped off his hat, and set it on the table next to him. Then he pushed off the jacket that had been slung over his shoulders and got to his feet. "I'm going upstairs. I'll be fine in the morning."

"Have you eaten anything?" Emma asked.

He made his way to the stairs. "I don't need anything to eat, Emma."

"Uh, Tucker—" Barry started tentatively. "The doc said you need to take these pills with food."

Tucker ran his hand over his forehead. "Sanchek, if I'd wanted a nurse, I would've brought one home with me."

Barry gave Emma a what-are-we-going-to-do-with-him kind of look.

Emma took the bag from Barry's hands. "I'll take care of him—whether he likes it or not."

As Tucker climbed the stairs, Barry grinned at her. "I was hoping you'd say that. I'm just glad *I'm* not the one who's trying to do it."

Emma was worried about Tucker but knew he wouldn't appreciate *her* concern anymore than he had Barry's. So after Barry left, she went to the kitchen, made a sandwich in record time, poured a glass of milk and took it upstairs with the pills, ready to do battle. She didn't knock on Tucker's bedroom door because she had her hands full. Pushing it open with her foot, she saw him sitting on the edge of the bed, trying to get out of his shirt. The expression on his face told her it wasn't an easy task.

Setting everything down on the night table, remembering exactly what had happened in this room the last time she was in it, she asked him, "Will you let me help you?"

The sling lay beside him on the bed. "Unfortunately," he said through almost clenched teeth, "I don't have much choice."

He'd unbuttoned his shirt and pulled it out of his trousers. Very carefully, she helped him slide out his good arm and then the one that was hurting him. Picking up the sling, she carefully put it over his head. But her hand brushed his good shoulder as she did, and he stared up at her. "I can handle this now."

Ignoring his protest, she reached for the sling, intending to help him get his arm into it. But he moved at the same time, and her fingers grazed his stomach.

"Emma, if you want to remain a virgin, I'd advise you to back off and back off *now*."

Startled, she let go of the sling. But then she gazed

squarely at him. "Maybe being a virgin isn't all it's cracked up to be."

Closing his eyes, he took a deep breath. "You can be the most trying woman."

"And you can be the most trying man. If you eat the sandwich and take the pills, I promise I'll leave you alone, except to look in on you every couple of hours."

"I don't have a concussion, just a bum shoulder," he growled.

"When you try to turn over in bed, you're going to want an ice pack, and one won't last you all night. So stop fighting me, Tucker. It's not going to do any good."

Exasperated with her, he let out a long breath. "You *could* just sleep with me. Then if I need something, you'll be right here."

"All right."

His eyes flew open, and then he smiled. "You would, wouldn't you?"

"I'd do whatever's best for you, Tucker."

He broke eye contact first and picked up half of the sandwich. After he ate it, he took the pill she'd placed on the dish. Finally, he muttered, "It's hard for me to accept help."

"I can see that. But you've helped me so much. You've given me so much. Let me just give a little bit back."

After a long, silent moment, he admitted, "I could use some help with my boots. And if you bring me an ice pack, I won't turn it away."

At that, Emma smiled at him and leaned down and kissed him on the cheek. "Don't go anywhere," she whispered. "I'll be right back with the ice pack."

She felt the heat of his gaze on her as she moved to the door. As she left his room, she hoped her feelings for him weren't one-sided. She hoped that just maybe he was a little bit in love with her, too.

On Wednesday, the twins were taking their nap and Emma took the opportunity to fold clean laundry and put it away. After she placed the towels in the linen closet, she carried Tucker's jeans and socks into his bedroom. She was glad his shoulder was healing. After that first night when she'd brought ice packs to him every few hours, he'd seemed more comfortable. He didn't like needing help, and she was pleased he'd finally accepted hers, at least for that one night. She could put his clothes on the bed as she usually did, but if she put them away, he wouldn't have to.

She found his jeans in the bottom drawer of the tall chest. T-shirts were in the drawer above that and socks were stacked in the drawer above that one. But they didn't take up the whole space and she saw a wooden picture frame lying on the right. Brushing his crew socks aside, she lifted out the photograph.

The picture was the type taken by a mall photographer with a colorful backdrop. The little boy was about three with dark eyes and hair. There was a quality about his smile that reminded her of Tucker's.

Who was this child?

His?

Would Tucker tell her if she asked?

A small voice in her heart told her it was too soon to ask. It was better if Tucker didn't know she'd seen it.

Removing the socks she'd dumped into the drawer, taking out the pair of jeans she'd folded into the other one, she laid all of it on Tucker's bed.

If he told her himself, she'd know he was letting her in. She was staying in his house, but she wanted to be an integral part of his life. The love of his life.

Couldn't dreams still come true?

Chapter Eight

The sound from the children's video playing in the living room drifted into the kitchen as Tucker calculated the value of the three jacks in his hand. He lifted his gaze, finally, to study the four other men at the table. Earl Grimes was stuffing a mini-quiche into his mouth instead of chewing on the butt of a cigar. Barry Sanchek was spreading chicken salad on a cracker. The improvement in the food offering had caught his attention right away. But Stan Coniff looked as if he was about ready to have a nicotine fit as he tapped his fingers on the table. He was a chain-smoker and used to a smoke-filled room when he played poker. Then there was Ed Barnes who kept glancing into the living room as if the happy sound of children's music was annoying. They'd been playing poker for the last hour and were all exceedingly aware that there were a woman and two kids in the next room, disrupting their usual game.

Tucker rotated his shoulder, which was now feeling

better, and realized this wasn't his usual life. Everything about it had changed since Emma had dropped into it.

Stan suddenly pushed back his chair. "I'm going outside for a smoke."

"You can't," Tucker said. "I'm raising you two bucks."

Stan blew out a breath. "Well, it's about time."

Suddenly Sammy came toddling into the kitchen and over to Tucker's chair.

A few seconds later, Emma was there scooping him up into her arms. "Sorry. He got away from me. Do you need refills on anything?"

Having a woman and children at a poker game just didn't seem fitting. Tucker shook his head. "We're fine." Steffie had crawled into the kitchen after Emma, and now *she* pulled herself up beside Tucker, too, grinning at him, with one finger poked into the side of her mouth.

Ed asked, "Is it their bedtime soon?"

Emma looked disconcerted and cast a questioning glance at Tucker. He knew Ed was just irritated because this was supposed to be a guys' night out—no women, no kids. "It is their bedtime, isn't it?" he asked Emma.

"I'll get them a snack and take them upstairs."

It didn't take Emma long to pluck two bottles from the refrigerator and open a box of zwieback cookies. Yet the presence of her and the twins in the kitchen had the men laying down their hands and waiting for her to finish.

"I'll take Steffie up and then come back down for Sammy. It'll just take a minute." When she leaned down to pick up the little girl, Tucker caught the scent of Emma's perfume, got a good view of the sweet curve of her backside, and had the sudden urge to pull her onto his lap. He must be losing his mind. He was in the middle of a poker game and thinking about kissing her!

Stan said, "I'm going out for that smoke."

Barry asked, "Anyone need another beer?" as he got up and went to the refrigerator.

By the time Emma returned downstairs, cuddled Sammy in her arms, gave them all a smile and left again, all of the men looked relieved. But less than fifteen minutes later, the sound of a wail came from upstairs, and Tucker guessed that one of the twins just didn't want to go to bed.

Then they both started fussing.

The men pretended to keep their mind on the game, but their glances went upstairs, and finally Earl asked Tucker, "How long is she staying with you?"

"Until we find her sister," he stated. That put an end to that conversation.

Even after Emma settled the twins down and no noise came from the second floor, the men still didn't banter and joke as they usually did. They bid and played their hands, but not with their usual enthusiasm, until around ten o'clock when they dispersed with excuses about why they had to leave early. Barry was the last one to leave, and before he opened the door he said, "Don't take it personally, Tucker. The guys always looked forward to your night for the game because you really *had* a bachelor's pad. But we'll find Josie Douglas. Maybe next time around, things will be back to normal.

Normal.

Tucker looked around the kitchen. There were clean baby bottles sitting on the counter and a stack of bibs next to them. He couldn't find anything in his cupboards, except maybe his dishes, because Emma had rearranged all of them. A children's gate sat propped against the refrigerator. In the living room, not only were there toys scattered across the floor, but three stacks of clothes sat on the sofa. Emma had been sorting them for the Thrift Shop. She seemed to try to take responsibility for everyone and everything.

As he turned away from the signs of how different his life had become to put away the leftover food, he heard Emma on the steps. A few moments later, she was standing in the kitchen in her nightgown and robe. Just what he needed right now...a vision to take to bed with him that would keep him awake all night.

"I'm sorry I couldn't get the twins to settle down sooner. They seemed to sense there was a party going on down here, and they wanted to be part of it."

"Not much of a party was going on tonight," he muttered.

"Was there something wrong with the food? With the kind of beer I bought?"

"It had nothing to do with the food and the beer." He tried to keep his eyes away from the soft swell of her breasts, from the creamy skin at her neckline.

"What was the problem then?"

"Emma, a guys' night out is supposed to be a guys' night out. They came here to get away from kids and wives. Usually my place is a...a haven. But it wasn't tonight because my life's not my own anymore."

Her silence told him he'd been too honest. Then she gave him a dose of honesty of her own. "Just what kind of life did you have, Tucker, living here by yourself?"

That sounded like a judgment, and the last thing he needed was somebody judging him. He'd done that for far too long himself. "A quiet one," he concluded with a hard stare.

She clasped her hands in front of her. "I see. So you prefer quiet to children's laughter, or to meaningful conversation with another adult, or to caring for someone and having them care back.''

"Listen, Emma—''

"I have listened, Tucker. I guess you prefer loneliness to really *having* a life. Children and responsibilities do take over. But that's what life's about.''

Suddenly having Emma and the twins in his house, knowing they weren't his and never would be, remembering everything he once had and lost, he felt old anger rise and surface once more. "Don't you tell *me* about responsibilities. I know more about them than most people.''

"How, Tucker? Does it have something to do with the picture of the little boy in your sock drawer?''

Overwhelming silence lay heavy between them. "Just how did you find that picture? Were you snooping?'' he growled.

"I wasn't snooping. I was putting away your socks so you didn't have to do it.''

"You had no business looking at it, let alone asking about it.''

She came a step closer. "Why shouldn't I ask, Tucker? I care about you. I care about who you are and who you've been. But you won't talk about it. Why won't you ever talk about your marriage?''

"Because there's nothing to talk about.'' His voice rose with each word.

Instead of responding in kind, she asked softly, "What happened, Tucker?''

"You want to know what happened so badly, I'll tell you what happened. I lost my son *and* my wife, and I never intend to care that much again.'' He knew the depth of his pain was in his eyes, on his face, in his voice, but he couldn't hide it now.

"What do you mean, you lost them?"

Before he realized he'd never discussed this with an-other living soul, he rushed to get it over with. "Denise hated my work as an undercover cop. But I told myself it was necessary work. I told myself my father would be proud of what I was doing, and that was as important to me as her opinion was."

He shook his head, knowing he'd deceived himself. "After Chad was born, our marriage seemed better for awhile. Or at least it was when I wasn't on assignments that took me away for a couple of days at a time. It got to the point we didn't even talk about it. There was more silence than talking. And on one of my last assignments, I didn't check in with Denise as I usually did. I couldn't, really—we were waiting for the bust to go down. But she'd tried to reach me. She'd left a message I never got. Chad had gotten sick. She ended up taking him to the hospital in the middle of the night and he was diagnosed with meningitis. By the time I *did* get the message and reached the hospital, he'd died. Three years old. Because my job meant more to me than my marriage. I wasn't there when my family needed me. Denise blamed me for that and so did I. Our marriage didn't survive it."

"Tucker..."

"I don't want your pity, Emma. You asked me about my marriage and the picture you found. Well, now you know all about it. I'm going out for a drive. I'll clean this up when I come home."

Then he snatched his jacket and hat from the wall rack and walked away before she could say another word...before she could judge him as harshly as he'd judged himself. When he went into the garage, he started up the SUV. Then he backed out, not knowing where he was going or how long he'd be gone. He just knew he couldn't face Emma again right now. He couldn't face the sleeping twins in his upstairs.

Because over the years he'd faced what he'd lost, and he was never going to feel that kind of pain again.

The following day Emma worried about Tucker as she cared for the twins, worked on her computer during their nap time, and then prepared supper. She'd heard him come in last night around 2:00 a.m. But he'd left this morning around six o'clock. She wasn't sure what she was going to say when she saw him again. She wasn't sure what she was going to do. He was hurting…had been for years. At times it seemed she and the twins added to that pain.

Last night's revelation had made her so sad. Not just for Tucker, but also because she'd realized something. Although she'd fallen in love with *him,* he'd never let himself fall in love with *her.*

When he called around four o'clock, she was happy to hear his voice, even though it was gruff when he said, "I won't be home for supper, Emma."

She wished she knew if work was keeping him away— or the thought of facing her. They'd have to talk eventually, whether he wanted to or not. Apparently he'd kept everything bottled up inside for too long. He thought locking it away was the best way to handle it. She knew better. But she didn't push him. Instead she responded, "That's okay, Tucker. I'm making a pot of soup. It'll be here when you get home." The implication was that she would be, too, if he wanted her to be.

After a quick thanks, he hung up. She had to give him space. She had to let him lead the way into his heart…if there was room for her with all the regrets and bittersweet memories.

It was nine o'clock, and she'd just gotten both twins settled for the night when she heard noise downstairs. Tucker was moving around in the kitchen. The microwave beeped. Stopping in her room, she brushed her hair and took a deep breath, then went downstairs.

To her surprise, Tucker wasn't in the kitchen eating supper, but rather sitting on the sofa with a cup of black coffee in front of him. Beside the coffee sat a mug of herbal tea. He'd also put a few muffins and cookies on a plate and placed them there, too.

"What's this?" she asked softly.

"I thought maybe you could use a cup of tea after a day with the twins."

She often made herself tea after she'd put the twins to bed. Apparently he'd noticed that. "Thank you."

There was an electric tension between them as she went around the coffee table and sat on the sofa next to him, careful not to sit too close.

After she played with her tea bag for a few moments, then finally took it out of the mug and set it on the small dish he'd provided for her muffins and cookies, she asked, "Did you have supper?"

"I wasn't hungry."

Studying him closely, she saw the lines of fatigue around his eyes, the soberness of his expression. He'd taken off his tie and unbuttoned the top buttons of his shirt. Brown hair curled there. He was such a strong man, yet right now, he looked like a man who was tired of carrying a burden.

But instead of talking about it, he said, "I have some good news."

"About Josie?"

He frowned and shook his head. "No, not yet. Remember the man who thought you might be his daughter?"

"Mr. Franz?"

"Yes."

"She finally called him. Roy thought we'd like to know. Apparently they're at least talking again. And she's going to come home at Christmas for a visit."

Christmas. If only Josie would come home for Christmas. It was a little over three weeks away.

"I know what you're thinking, Emma," Tucker said gently. "Maybe Josie will call you before we find her. She can't help but think about her twins at Christmas if she's any kind of mother at all."

"Unless something happened to her. Unless..."

Tucker covered her hand with his. "Don't go there."

Trying to keep her fears in check, she took a deep breath, loving the feel of his hand on hers, knowing she had to bring up last night. "Tucker, about last night—"

He shook his head.

But she kept going anyway. "I'm sorry I invaded your privacy."

"You didn't deserve that outburst. I'm the one who's sorry." Looking deeply into her eyes he went on, "You've brought excitement and caring and tenderness back into my life."

His words warmed her, but she knew they had to talk about his loss. "I'm so sorry about your wife and child."

Uncovering her hand, he leaned forward, picked up his coffee mug and took a few sips. "I want to forget about it, Emma. Time has helped some. More time should help more."

She wasn't sure if the old saying that time healed all wounds was accurate. She also knew something had to start that healing process. If she and the twins could do that for Tucker—if her *love* could do that for Tucker—maybe there was hope. "If you ever want to talk, I'll listen."

Setting down his coffee mug, he moved a little closer to her and gazed down at her. "You're a good listener, but talking won't change anything."

Desperately she wanted to reach up to him, put her arms around him, and hold him tight. She wanted to give him all her love and let it heal him. "How can I help you, Tucker?"

"I don't need your help." Then a slow smile curved his lips. "But I do need your company, and I think we could both use a little fun. The police department in Omaha is sponsoring a dinner and dance. It's next Saturday night. Would you like to go?"

Dancing with Tucker. Being held in his arms. "I'd love to go with you."

He looked relieved. "Good. It's a pretty classy affair, held at one of the best hotels in Omaha."

She had a dress in her closet back home in Cedarton that would be perfect. It was long, crushed blue velvet. She had bought it on sale before Christmas one year to wear to her Christmas party at work. She'd only ever worn it that one time. "I'll have to go back to Cedarton to pick up a few things, but I've wanted to check on the house and make sure everything's okay. Even though Cal's keeping watch, I want to make sure myself."

"We could make it an outing tomorrow—take the twins, get what you need and have breakfast or brunch somewhere."

"Are you sure that's the way you want to spend your day off?"

He reached down and brushed her hair away from her cheek slowly. "I'm very sure." Then he leaned back and said, "You know what? I think I *am* hungry. I'm going to warm up some of that soup. Would you like anything?"

She wanted him to stay here and kiss her. She wanted him to tell her how much she meant to him. But instead, she looked forward to tomorrow and to next Saturday night. "No, I'm fine. Go ahead."

Staying close to her for a few seconds longer, as if that's what he wanted, too, he finally leaned away and then stood. When he went into the kitchen, Emma took a deep breath, looking forward to the next week... looking forward to spending more time with Tucker.

Sammy cried out around 2:00 a.m. and Tucker came awake instantly. He, too, had learned to distinguish the babies' cries, and this was definitely Sammy's. It was lower than Steffie's and huskier. Emma had put in a full day, working during the babies' nap time and then, also, this evening. She deserved to sleep through the night.

Quickly he opened his door and went over to the twins' room. Standing at Sammy's crib, he bent over him. "Hey, little guy. What's the problem? Is your diaper too wet?" He remembered yesterday and the contented feeling he'd had after spending the day with Emma and the twins in Cedarton.

Rolling to his knees, Sammy looked up at Tucker, pulled himself up by the crib rails and smiled.

Tucker chuckled. "I don't think anything's wrong at all. I just think you couldn't sleep, and you didn't want to be up alone. Well, let's not wake your sister." Lifting Sammy, he took him over to the changing table and checked his diaper. He was wet.

After Sammy was clean and dry, Tucker buttoned up

his sleeper, then lifted the little boy into his arms. He looked into Sammy's eyes and remembered another baby—another time. Sometimes it hurt so badly to be near the twins that he couldn't stand it. But he couldn't seem to stay away from them, either. The push-pull made his gut clench and caused turmoil that he didn't begin to know how to deal with. Yet holding Sammy now, his little body warm against Tucker's, he knew satisfaction as well as pain, and joy as well as sorrow.

Sammy didn't look as if he was ready to go back to bed, and Tucker knew if the little boy stayed awake, he'd soon have Steffie up, too. Going over to the rocker, Tucker settled in, positioning Sammy in the crook of his arm. Then keeping his voice low, he told him a story he used to tell Chad...about a little boy who ventured into a forest to find a treasure.

In the room next door, Emma wasn't quite sure why she came awake. Had one of the babies cried?

Then she heard the sound coming from the babies' room—the creaking of the floorboards as the rocker pressed on them. Slipping out of bed, she put on her robe, and then quietly went to the door and opened it. The glow of the night-light shone from the twins' room. Her bare feet were silent on the floor as she peeked inside.

The sight brought a smile to her lips and tears to her eyes. Tucker was tenderly holding Sammy, rocking him and talking to him in a low voice. It was almost indistinguishable. Emma knew it didn't matter what Tucker was saying to Sammy. His voice was steady and calming and soothing, and Sammy's eyes were half-closed. It was a moment in time she wouldn't soon forget, and she didn't want to disrupt it. Tucker was getting closer to the twins than he wanted to admit. They had the wonderful knack of winning your heart before you even knew it was happening. Emma suspected he wasn't immune to them—even though he might want to be.

Tucker Malone was a man who'd been born to be a father. He had the touch, and the voice, and the spirit to raise a child with patience and love. Why couldn't he see that? Why couldn't he see that he still had so much to give? Why couldn't he understand that if he opened himself up to love, the hurt would lessen, and maybe eventually even go away?

Yet she knew he wouldn't listen to her if she told him that. She knew he had to discover it on his own.

Stepping away from the door, she went back to her room, careful not to make any noise. When she settled in bed again and closed her eyes, she could still see Tucker rocking Sammy. Sheriff Tucker Malone was a good man. He was the man she loved. Maybe Saturday night she could tell him that. Maybe Saturday night, she could find out if he loved her, too.

When Emma descended the steps on Saturday evening, she saw Aunt Gertie sitting on the floor with the twins. The older woman wore jeans and a Dallas Cowboys sweatshirt, and no one could ever tell she was as old as she was—though no one knew her actual age because she wouldn't say.

"Well, well. Don't you look pretty?" the older woman observed as her gaze swept over Emma.

Emma had attempted to swirl all of her hair up into curls on top of her head, lacing a black velvet ribbon through them. But many of her curls had escaped, a few falling here and there, several down along her cheeks. She'd liked the effect and left them that way. The stand-up collar of her dress was edged in silver, and tiny, glittery buttons beginning at her neck fastened the dress down to her hemline. She carried a black suede purse to match her high heels and felt every bit as nervous as she felt dressed up.

Tucker entered the living room just then and stared at her as she came down the last few steps. The mesmerized expression on his face made her feel as if she'd done something right. Tucker, himself, looked more handsome than she'd ever seen him, in his charcoal suit and black-and-charcoal tie. His white dress shirt looked crisp, and she suspected the laundry had starched it.

He picked up the black velvet cape draped over the back of the armchair and held it for her. "This isn't very heavy. Are you sure you're going to be warm enough?"

With Tucker beside her, she'd be plenty warm. "I'll be fine," she assured him. As he laid the cape over her shoulders, his fingers brushed the nape of her neck and a delighted shiver went through her. This was going to be a special night. She knew it was.

After she'd buttoned the cape, she went over to Sammy and Steffie and gave them hugs and kisses, telling them good-night.

"We could be late," Tucker told Aunt Gertie.

"Don't you worry about that. I've fallen asleep on the couch pretty often in my lifetime. And I do appreciate you picking me up and taking me home. It's a little cold out there for my shopping cart."

Tucker smiled. "I thought it might be. I left the number of the hotel on the refrigerator. We'll be in the main ballroom."

Aunt Gertie waved her hand at him as she pulled Steffie onto her lap and gave her a little hug. "Don't you worry about us. We'll be just fine. The fact of the matter is—I'm looking forward to a little peace and quiet after these two go to bed. My house has been like Grand Central Station ever since my relatives arrived. I love them dearly, but it does get noisy at times. Now you two run along and start celebrating Christmas early.''

Tucker and Emma were in his truck and had left Storkville's traffic light behind them when he said, ''You really look beautiful tonight.''

She glanced at him in the shadows of the cab. ''Thank you. It's been a while since I dressed up.''

''Me, too,'' he admitted. ''I'd forgotten what a real tie feels like.''

She could sense his smile. ''I was afraid I'd forgotten how to walk in high heels.''

''It looks to me as if you know how to walk in them just fine.''

Her heart raced faster with the idea that he watched her moves, just as she watched his. For the past week Tucker hadn't seemed as guarded when he was around her. He'd played with Sammy and Steffie more often than he had in the past, too. She was hoping that now that the subject of his wife and son had been brought out into the light, the darkness around it would go away.

The last time they'd driven to Omaha, she hadn't known who she was or what was going to happen next. Now she still didn't know what was going to happen next, but she was sure of who she was, and that her love for Tucker was growing stronger each day. She couldn't imagine her life without him in it and didn't want to.

The ballroom of the Omaha Wellsley Hotel was filled with dark-suited men and finely dressed women. Tucker checked in with the hostess at a table inside the door, and then took Emma's cape from her and hung it on one of the coatracks. They'd been given seating cards and now looked for Table 9, finding it without much trouble. Three other couples were already seated there. The men rose and shook hands with Tucker, nodding to Emma, as everyone introduced themselves. As Emma began a conversation with the woman beside her, and Tucker with the man beside him, she was aware of being here as part of a couple. She liked the feeling. Her shoulder brushed his now and then. His elbow grazed hers.

Their fingers tangled as he passed the bread basket to her, and neither of them pulled away. Tucker's gaze met Emma's. When she smiled at him, he smiled back. It was as if they had run away for a night—to an adventure that was theirs and theirs alone.

They had finished crème de menthe parfaits and were sipping coffee when the lights dimmed and a band began to play. A male vocalist started to sing a slow, popular ballad, and Tucker asked Emma, "Would you like to dance?"

She nodded.

As they excused themselves from the table, Tucker rested his hand at her waist. They threaded their way through tables, and it stayed there, sending a tingling awareness of him throughout her body.

Several couples were already dancing. Tucker took her into his arms, holding her loosely. "I haven't danced in a long while," he murmured. "This could be dangerous for you."

She looked up into his dark brown eyes and knew the danger came from losing her heart irrevocably to him. "I haven't done this very often. I learned in high school in physical education class. That was about it."

"Then we'll keep it simple," he said, pulling her a little closer, bringing her hand into his chest.

Their feet made a simple box to the rhythm and their movements seemed totally natural, as if they'd danced together many times before.

She could feel his large hand through the material of her dress as she laid her cheek on his shoulder. He was wearing cologne tonight, something that smelled like spruce and spice. She could feel the power in his legs as he guided her, the tautness of his chest as she lay against him. Everything about Tucker was strong and steady and, as she lifted her head and gazed up into his eyes, she again saw the fire there. He'd brought her tonight to get closer to her, and she'd accepted the invitation to get closer to him—in all ways.

The dim lights, the slow music, their movement in the shadows, set the atmosphere for intimacy. She loved having his arms around her. She loved breathing in his scent. She loved feeling safe and feminine whenever she was with him. When he bent his head, she didn't hesitate to give him her lips. She didn't hesitate to kiss him back, letting him take it deeper, letting him arouse her, as she could tell he was aroused.

One song faded into the next until he wrapped his arms around her and they simply swayed to the music. Their bodies fit together so perfectly that words weren't necessary.

She lost track of time and space and everything, except the desire in Tucker's eyes, the sensuality of his fingers, the heat of his kiss.

Finally he broke one of their many kisses to trail his lips across her cheek and down her neck. His breathing was ragged, and so was hers, and she could feel his need as tangibly as her own.

Leaning his forehead against hers, he said, "I want you, Emma."

As she gazed into his eyes, she knew she was making one of the most important statements of her life. "I want you, too."

Waiting for his response, she held her breath.

Chapter Nine

"Let's get a room." Tucker's voice was husky and deep.

Emma looked into his eyes and knew she wanted to make love with him, as much as he wanted to make love with her. "All right."

"Do you want to wait at the table while I go to the lobby?"

"No. I'll come with you." She wasn't ashamed of wanting to be with Tucker. "Besides, they might not have a room."

Draping his arm around her, he muttered, "Then we'll go to another hotel."

It didn't take much time at all to find out the hotel *did* have vacant rooms, and they checked into one. Tucker kept glancing at her throughout the process. She gave him a smile, and her stomach fluttered at what she was about to do. When they found themselves alone in the elevator, Tucker took her into his arms and kissed her again. The elevator doors opened and they broke apart, stepping out.

He took her hand as they walked to the room, and she felt so happy that she decided she could float there. After he used the key, he let her precede him inside. She watched him put the Do Not Disturb sign on the outside doorknob, and then he came to her.

Taking her cape from over her arm, her purse from her hand, he laid them on the luggage rack. "From the moment you came down those stairs tonight, Emma, I wanted to be alone with you. I've wanted to be alone with you for weeks."

"We're alone now," she whispered.

When he came to her once again, he took her face in his hands and kissed her so tenderly, so hungrily, so desperately, she wanted to cry. Their need was mutual, but since she'd never done this before, she let him lead. As he kissed her, his fingers undid the buttons of her dress. Stopping at her waist, he brushed the velvet from her shoulders and let it fall to the floor. She wore a silky bra and a long slip, and he stared at her as if she were something too beautiful to touch.

"Can I undress *you?*" she asked.

He groaned and shook his head. "That's a dangerous thing to ask a man, Emma. It's as arousing as hell."

"Or heaven?" she suggested sweetly.

Laughing, he shrugged out of his suit jacket and tossed it over her cape. "Go ahead," he said, "and we'll see if we can't get to heaven together."

It didn't take her long to tug open his tie and unbutton and remove his shirt. But after she did, she tentatively touched his chest, and then flattened her palms against the curly, brown hair. He sucked in a breath and took her hands into his, kissing her fingertips. "I've never wanted anyone as much as I want you."

Knowing Tucker, she knew that wasn't a line. His honesty and integrity guided everything he did and said.

Slowly he brought her to him, then kissed her long, and deep, and hard, taking the pins and ribbon from her hair, running his hands through it. "Your hair is so silky and soft. Like you."

His next kiss led them to the bed, where he unfastened her bra and she unbuckled his belt. When Tucker touched her breasts, her fingers froze, and every nerve in her body came alive with his touch...tingled...heated...until she knew she'd never forget this experience as long as she lived. He bent his head to her breast and touched her nipple with his tongue. She felt the coiling deep inside of her—tighter and tighter and tighter—pleasurable and erotic, yet yearning and hungry, too.

"Oh, Tucker, I never felt like this before. I never imagined it could be like this. I want you to make love to me—"

The sudden change in his expression stopped her, and she wondered what she'd said or what she'd done wrong. The sparks of desire were still in his eyes, but his mouth tightened into a line. "I don't want you to have any illusions about this, Emma. This doesn't have anything to do with love or dreams or the future. This is about us, and now, and the pleasure we can give each other. I thought you understood that."

She was beginning to understand all too clearly—not only what tonight was about, but what she meant to him. Before she jumped to conclusions, she had to ask, "You're not interested in making love with me? You just want to have sex? That's what tonight's all about?"

He sat up. "That's what tonight's about. Getting dressed up, enjoying a little foreplay on the dance floor..."

"Foreplay? Tucker, I thought we were—" Her voice caught, but this time she wouldn't let him see her emotions. She wouldn't let him see how much he was hurting her. Grabbing her bra from where it lay on the bed, she quickly slipped it on. "I guess you were right, Tucker. Maybe I *am* innocent, or maybe I'm just gullible. I thought you really cared about me, and tonight was about that."

"Emma—"

"Would you mind waiting for me downstairs in the lobby?" she asked, needing to get him out of the room before she started crying.

After a tense moment, he slid his legs over the side of the bed and stood. "Sure. No problem."

It seemed like only a minute until he had his shirt on, his tie slung around his neck, and he'd shrugged into his jacket. "At least we stopped in time. At least we didn't make a mistake we couldn't undo." When she didn't respond, he said, "I'll be waiting for you in the lobby."

After he'd left the room and closed the door behind him, Emma felt like screaming, or throwing something, or having an absolute temper tantrum. But instead, tears filled her eyes and rolled down her cheeks. She *had* made a mistake she couldn't undo. She'd given her heart to him, and he'd as much as said he didn't want it.

For a few minutes, she took deep, calming breaths, then went to the bathroom and washed her face with cold water. She'd taken responsibility for herself all of her life, and she had depended on no one. She'd been wrong to think she could now.

She had plenty of thinking to do tonight, and by tomorrow morning, she'd have a new plan for her life…one that didn't include Tucker Malone.

* * *

When Emma awakened on Sunday morning, she knew something was wrong. Then she remembered. Last night. Tucker. The hotel room.

With a heavy heart she relived their icily silent ride home. There just hadn't been anything to say. She certainly couldn't tell him she loved him. Not when all he wanted from her was pleasure.

Checking the clock, she saw that it was 7:00 a.m. Maybe she could get an hour's work in at the computer before the twins awakened. Maybe that would keep her mind off of Tucker and the decisions she had to make. She dressed quickly, and when she went downstairs, Tucker's door was still closed.

A half hour later, she was staring at the site on the monitor when she sensed Tucker's presence. She looked up and saw him in the doorway. He was wearing his uniform, which was odd for Sunday. "Going to work?" she asked lightly.

"I have to pick up some papers at the office and then I'm driving to the Cedar County Jail. I have a meeting with your mugger and his lawyer."

"Why?"

"Because I found out some things about him. He's not your usual thief. He's basically a family man who lost his job and didn't know which way to turn. He wouldn't accept charity or handouts but didn't know to feed his family and pay his bills. Believe it or not, pool hustling has been getting him by for the most part. The muggings were desperate attempts to keep on going. He doesn't have a record and has never been in trouble before. So I'm thinking about making some recommendations to the D.A."

Tucker was such a good man—a caring man. Yet he wouldn't let himself care enough to change his life. "I hope your meeting goes well.'' She leaned back in her chair, debated with herself for a few moments, and then decided to plunge in. ''Tucker, I've been thinking. I think I should go back to Cedarton.''

His jaw tensed. ''Because you think it's time? Or because of what happened last night?''

''Because of what happened last night.''

He stared out the window for a few moments, then brought his gaze back to hers. ''The reason you're staying here hasn't changed. I haven't found Josie, and you'd be alone up there with no help. Don't make a decision about this now. Think about it till I get back, and we'll talk then. Okay?''

This morning she couldn't tell the sheriff from the man. She didn't know if he was just being practical, or if he really cared if she left. Maybe she *was* still too upset to make a good decision. A few more hours wouldn't hurt.

Suddenly Emma heard noises coming from the baby monitor she'd brought with her into the den. Sammy was awake and she was sure it wouldn't be long before Steffie was, too. Standing, she crossed to the doorway, but Tucker didn't move. He just stood there, looking down at her.

''I have to get the babies up.''

''Will you be gone by the time I get back?'' he asked.

''No. We'll talk about it again later.''

He looked as if he wanted to say more. He looked as if he wanted to do something, like kiss her. But that was out of the question now that she knew how he felt.

Stepping aside, he let her pass. ''I should be home by midafternoon. Page me if you need me.''

That was the problem. She was trying *not* to need him.

Fortunately Sammy and Steffie's noises became louder. She murmured, "See you later" and went to the stairs.

Tucker didn't say goodbye before he left, and she felt like crying all over again.

The day passed slowly, and even Sammy and Steffie seemed to be unsettled. Sammy was particularly fussy and she decided he was teething again, and just tried to keep him happy any way she could. But simply looking around Tucker's house made her heart ache. She'd thought about decorating it for Christmas. Helping him put up the tree they'd tagged...

She tried to dismiss her dream and tried to think about returning to Cedarton as she settled Sammy and Steffie for their afternoon naps. But life in Cedarton seemed so...barren compared to life in Storkville. She'd made friends here, and so had the twins.

After she put a cup of water in the microwave to make herself tea, she opened the freezer and took out a pack of ground meat for supper. But as she contemplated what she wanted to do with it, the doorbell rang. Maybe it was Camille dropping off more clothes for the Thrift Shop. Emma had sorted at least ten boxes that were now stacked in the garage.

When she opened the front door, her mouth dropped open and she just stared. It was Josie! Her straight, auburn hair was down to her shoulders now. Her big, green eyes looked sad and fearful. She was wearing jeans and her parka—

Her sister's presence finally registered, and Emma threw her arms around her, giving her a huge, tight hug. "Oh, my heavens! It's you! Are you all right? I've been so worried."

At Josie's silence, Emma leaned away and saw that her sister was crying. Putting her arm around her, Emma drew her inside. Emma had so many questions, but she didn't want Josie to run again. She needed to know what was going on in her head.

Before they went deeper into the living room, Josie took a tissue from her pocket and blew her nose. "I've got so much to tell you. I'm so sorry for leaving the way I did, but I didn't know what else to do. What are you doing here? In your note, you said this was Tucker Malone's house. Who's he? And do you know where the twins are?" she rushed on. "I left them at the day-care center. But if you're here, maybe you know that—"

"Take your coat off and come sit with me," Emma suggested softly, "and we'll talk about everything. The twins are upstairs sleeping."

"They're *here?*"

At Josie's amazed expression, Emma sighed. "It's a long story."

Josie glanced around nervously. "Is this Mr. Malone here now?"

"No. He's the Sheriff of Cedar County, Josie."

Her sister looked terrified and covered her face with her hands. "Oh my gosh. I knew it. I'm in all kinds of trouble. Is he going to arrest me? Maybe I shouldn't stay." But then she looked up the stairs. "But I have to see Sammy and Steffie. I've been away from them for so long."

Emma drew Josie over to the sofa and they sat. After Josie shrugged off her coat, she asked, "Do you think they'll still remember me?"

"I know they will. Tell me why you ran away," Emma beseeched her. "Tell me why you didn't leave the twins with me."

"It was such a mess," her sister said.

"Start at the beginning."

Josie pushed her bangs up her forehead. It was a gesture Emma knew well. Her sister always did that when she was upset. "I met this man when I was working at the McCormack Estate. He was a lot older than I was, but he *really* seemed to like me. He was kind and gentle and *so* charming. He treated me like I've never been treated before...by anyone. He made me feel beautiful and wanted—like I was important, not a screwup. Do you know what I mean?"

"I know what you mean," Emma assured her.

"The only thing was," Josie went on, "he didn't want anyone to know about us. He said it was more romantic to keep our relationship a secret. And that was okay with me. I just wanted to be with him, not with anyone else— like his family, or anything. He even took me to this private dining room at Chez Stork. You know, where no one else knows you're there? It was *so* cool."

Emma guessed that Tucker's suspicions about Jackson Caldwell Sr. being the father of the twins was correct. But she wanted Josie to tell her herself. "How long did you see him?"

"About three months or so and then..." She took a breath. "He broke up with me. He said I was getting too serious. I thought we were going to get married, but he told me he wasn't interested in marriage. He only wanted to have some fun. Oh, Em, it was so hard not seeing him anymore. And then a few weeks later I found out I was pregnant. When I tried to call him, his housekeeper told me he was out of the country."

She shook her head as tears rolled down her cheeks. "I called week after week, but he wasn't there or else he just didn't take my calls. The last time I tried to reach him was the night before Sammy and Steffie were born.

Then after I had them, I decided if he didn't want me, I didn't want him."

The defiance left her face as she clasped her hands tightly in her lap. "Then we had Sammy and Steffie to take care of…day and night…all the time. It was like a twenty-four-hour jail sentence. I felt so trapped. And I kept getting these letters from Mindy Patterson. Do you remember Mindy? We were in high school together. She left Cedarton right after high school and ended up in Kearney. She had her own apartment and everything, and a great job, working for an insurance company. She told me to come visit her anytime I wanted. She knew all these cool guys."

Emma's heart ached for Josie. She was still a child, trying to become an adult and not knowing how. Emma felt guilty about that. If she'd done something differently…

"Remember that week in August when it rained?" Josie asked. "And Sammy and Steffie wouldn't sleep? We were up for hours with them every night."

"I remember."

"Then that storm took the shingles off the roof. And Cal was away. And you had to pay somebody to fix it. You said you had to redo the budget, that the expenses were going to be higher for winter. And I…I just got tired of seeing you trying to scrimp and get by, and both of us being tired, and you working, too. It all just seemed like too much for both of us. You'd been making sacrifices all your life for me, and then for the babies. I was so tired of being a burden to you, Em."

"Josie…"

"You can *say* I wasn't, but I was. I decided the first thing I should do was make Sammy and Steffie's father take responsibility for them. I thought we could move in with him for awhile. I decided to just show up on his doorstep, and somebody would have to deal with us. But when I got to his house, nobody answered and a man walking by the house told me that he'd *died* four months before!''

"The man was Jackson Caldwell, Sr.," Emma concluded.

"How did you know?"

"Tucker's a good sheriff. He's been doing some investigating. He thought it might be Quentin McCormack for awhile, though, because of the rattle he found with Sammy. Did you take that?"

Josie blushed. "I didn't intend to. I was filling in for a maid right after I found out I was pregnant. I was dusting the upstairs rooms and went into one that was for babies. Oh, Em. It was beautiful. And I knew I could never provide my babies with that kind of furniture, that kind of tradition. So I went over to these shelves, and the rattle was there, and I just picked it up and was looking at it... Just kind of wishing for something I couldn't have, I guess. Then that butler, Mr. Harriman, came up checking on things and he saw me there. So I just slipped it into my pocket, planning to put it back. But I never got the chance. I never meant to keep it. It just sort of happened."

That was the problem with Josie. Things just sort of happened to her. "Why did you leave the twins at the day-care center?"

"I kept remembering Mindy's letters. The life she had—the dates, the job, the money. And I'd heard about how everyone in Storkville loves children and babies, and the new day-care center. I don't know what happened. I just wanted someone else to take care of them for a while. I wanted to get away and find out what life was really like. So I left them there. I knew they'd be well taken care of.''

"Oh, Josie."

"Did you come here and find them? Is that what happened? I bet they've grown so big."

Emma wasn't sure exactly where to start. "After your phone call, I searched your room for clues, and I found a matchbook with your name and Jack's written in a heart. Since the matchbook came from the General Store here, that's where I was going to look first. But it was late in the day when I arrived. I decided to see if the bed-and-breakfast had a room. I'd check in, then go to the diner and start asking questions. I never expected you to just leave the babies somewhere..."

Josie dropped her eyes to her lap but mumbled, "Not just anywhere. I knew BabyCare would be a good place."

Emma decided not to pursue that for the moment. Rather, she said, "I never got to the bed-and-breakfast. I was mugged."

Josie's chin shot up and she stared at Emma.

Emma told her sister about the amnesia, about staying with Aunt Gertie, and finally moving in with Tucker at the end of October.

Emma ended with, "So he expected you were around Kearney, but didn't know how to find you. I didn't know Mindy Patterson had moved there. You never told me that. You never told me a lot of things."

Josie hung her head in guilty silence, but then asked, "Can I see Sammy and Steffie?"

"First, answer me one question, honey. What brought you back?"

"Lots of things. The car broke down right after I got there, and I didn't have the money to get it fixed. I didn't want anybody to trace me there, and I knew if I got a regular job that would happen. So I began working for a friend of Mindy's—an interior decorator who needed someone to go along to houses with her, carry sample books, and I saved up money. I finally got the car fixed about two weeks ago, and I managed to save some cash. I brought it along for you, if you need it, if Sammy and Steffie need anything.''

''We don't need anything. Just you.''

Tears welled up in Josie's eyes again, and Emma hugged her once more. Then they went upstairs.

The twins were sleeping peacefully. Josie leaned over each one, letting her fingers slide along Sammy's cheek and then Steffie's. ''They've grown.''

''Not only that, but Sammy's walking now,'' Emma said in a low voice.

As they stood staring down at the babies, Emma heard the garage door open. A few moments later, she heard Tucker's steps downstairs. And, as he usually did, he came looking for her.

''Is that him?'' Josie asked, looking as if she wanted to run.

By the time Emma answered yes, Tucker was standing in the doorway. ''I saw the car in the driveway,'' he stated, ''and the license plate.''

''Tucker, this is my sister, Josie Douglas. Josie, Tucker Malone.''

Tucker's expression was stern. ''So you came back. What are you going to do about the twins? Are you finally going to take responsibility for them?''

Before Josie began crying again, Emma wrapped her arm around her and gave Tucker a reproving glare. ''Josie just got here and has been explaining everything that happened to her. I know you want to talk about all that, but I think she needs to get something to eat and rest a little bit first. Josie, why don't you go down to the kitchen and make a pot of tea. I'll be down in a few minutes.''

But Tucker wouldn't be put off that easily. ''We're going to have to notify Judge Peabody that she's back. He'll want to set up a meeting. Miss Douglas, I recommend that you don't do anything rash at least for the next few days. It's probably best if you stay here until we get this all settled.''

Emma knew Tucker was warning Josie. He was warning Emma, too. If Josie did anything stupid again, she was going to have to pay the consequences. He wanted to keep an eye on her, and what better way to do that, but to have her under his roof, too. It did make sense. Until they all decided what would happen next.

When Josie glanced at Emma, Emma nodded her head. ''It might be better if you stay here. You can sleep with me. It'll be like old times.''

''For how long?'' she asked.

''Until we meet with the judge, and he decides what he's going to do about custody of the twins.''

Josie looked very young and very uncertain. Then she took a last look at Sammy and Steffie. ''I'll wait for you downstairs.''

Emma followed her sister into the hall and waited until she went down and into the kitchen. Then she turned to Tucker. ''Ease up.''

''Ease up? And let her do what she damned well pleases again?''

They were standing at the top of the steps, but Emma didn't want to invite him into her room—and she certainly wasn't going into his with him. The snap and crackle between them was still too strong.

''Your sister has caused a lot of people worry and

expense over the past two-and-a-half months,'' he continued. ''It's time she takes responsibility for her own life. You need one of your own. You've never had one. Just maybe, that's what your amnesia was all about.''

''Don't be ridiculous.''

''I'm not being ridiculous. It's what the doctor suggested, and you know it. You've had responsibilities all your life, Emma. You weren't much more than a child when your parents died. Don't you want a break?''

Facing him squarely, Emma answered, ''You can't take a break from people you love. Especially when they need you.''

''Too much need isn't healthy,'' he shot back.

''Not needing at all isn't healthy, either,'' she retorted, barely aware of the creak of floorboards on the first floor, thinking it was just the sounds of the house settling in the cold temperature.

After a prolonged silence, Tucker finally asked, ''Are you going to convince her to stay here with you?''

''That probably would be best until we see the judge. But Tucker, please don't treat her like a criminal. Okay? She's my sister, and I love her.'' She loved him, too, and she so wanted to tell him that. But nothing about his attitude said he wanted to hear it.

''I'll try to remember that,'' he said gruffly. ''But she's got to realize there are consequences for everything she does. If you don't point that out to her, I will.'' Then he went down the stairs and she followed him, with the sinking feeling in her heart that she was going to be acting as a buffer for the next few days. After that, she'd probably be leaving his house and his life.

The next few days were filled with all kinds of simmering tension that was always just below the surface.

Their meeting with the judge was scheduled for the following Monday. Judge Peabody was simply too busy to see them before that. In the meantime, Emma felt it was best if Josie spent as much time as possible with the twins. But after a couple of hours of being with them, Josie would back off, saying she was going for a walk or to the General Store. Emma didn't want her to feel like a prisoner, so she took over then. But she felt Tucker's disapproval when she did.

A short time after Josie had arrived, Emma had called Aunt Gertie to come over and meet her sister. Josie had taken to the older lady, listening to her tales of her life in Storkville when she was a young girl. Aunt Gertie didn't seem to be judging Josie, and Josie could tell that. Emma had also called Cal, and Tucker had spoken with Jackson who had assured him he and Hannah would be waiting to hear what the judge decided.

Finally on Friday morning, Emma realized the only way to give Josie complete responsibility for the twins was if she left the house and put her in charge. Sammy was stuffy this morning and his nose was running. But Emma decided he would be all right without her for a few hours.

At breakfast, Emma told Josie, "It's time you care for the twins on your own. I'm going to help out in the Thrift Shop today. The deputies' wives are getting the store ready to open next week. If you need anything, I've left the Thrift Shop number on the refrigerator, as well as Aunt Gertie's number, the day-care center number— where she probably is if she isn't home, and Tucker's number."

"You want me to take care of the twins all by myself?"

"You're their mother, Josie."

With Josie looking very uncertain, Emma patted her hand. "I know you can do it, and *you* need to know you can do it so the judge hears that confidence in you when he questions you."

"Maybe we should wait longer to see him. Maybe..."

"It's not a trial, honey. It's just a conference. It'll be okay."

But Emma worried after she left the house. She worried all day.

It was late morning when Cal called her at the Thrift Shop. "How did you know I was here?" she asked him.

"Josie told me."

Maybe Cal could tell from his conversation with Josie what was happening at the house. "How's she doing?"

"She sounded a bit flustered—had to get off the phone."

That added to Emma's worry. Maybe she should leave early. Maybe she should go back to Tucker's and help her sister. But then her resolve took over again. Josie had to know she could take care of the twins.

Bringing her attention back to Cal, she asked, "Are you calling to check up on me?"

"Actually, I want you to meet someone."

"Who?"

"Her name's Bonnie Arkin. She's a trucker I met in California. She arrived for Thanksgiving and is staying with me for a little while. I thought maybe the four of us could go to dinner. You know—you and Tucker, me and Bonnie. How's tomorrow night?"

She wasn't sure Tucker wanted to go anywhere with her, least of all on a double date. But she did want to meet this lady friend of Cal's. There was excitement in his voice that she hadn't heard before. "I have no idea what Tucker's schedule's like. I'll talk to him and get back to you. Okay? And, even if he can't come, maybe the three of us could go to dinner.''

"Is everything all right?" Cal asked.

"Everything's muddled. Josie. Tucker. Josie and I will probably be moving back to Cedarton soon. I'll give you a call tonight or tomorrow.''

After Cal insisted she call him if she needed him, she hung up, still thinking about Josie alone with the twins—still worrying.

As Josie fed the twins lunch, she'd never seen such a mess. And she'd never felt so frazzled in all of her life. At least Steffie was eating. Sammy wasn't. He wouldn't eat and he wouldn't drink. His nose was running and he was coughing a little, but just a little. Emma knew his nose was running. She would have known if he should go to the doctor or not.

Josie offered him a spoonful of applesauce but he just wouldn't take it. Then he rammed his hand into the dish and spilled it all over the tray and himself. Josie just stared at the mess. The pudding that Emma had made was all over Steffie. The floor was a disaster with its toys and plastic containers and spills.

She couldn't do this. She couldn't handle this.

Ever since she'd gotten here on Sunday, Sheriff Malone had been looking at her as if she were a criminal. He wanted answers, and she didn't have any. Everything that had made her want to run in August made her want to run again. But she knew she couldn't cause Emma that worry.

Still, she needed a little space. Maybe Aunt Gertie would watch the kids for a few hours. She was homesick for Cedarton—at least she thought she was. If she went back there, was in her own room, maybe she'd finally figure out what she really wanted...what she had to do. She'd heard Emma and Tucker arguing about her on Sunday. He'd insisted she had to take responsibility for her own life.

Going to the refrigerator, she took the slip of paper from under the magnet that had all the phone numbers on it. Then she dialed Aunt Gertie's number.

The Thrift Shop took shape as Betty and Camille and Emma worked hard to tag items, make displays eye-catching, and learn how to use the cash register. They'd hired a staff, but they also knew they'd be helping out now and then. It was almost five o'clock and they were admiring their handiwork when the phone rang. Camille picked it up and then held it out to Emma. "It's Tucker. He sounds...strange."

Emma took the cordless phone from Camille. "Tucker, what is it?"

"It's Sammy. I came home to check on things, and Gertie was here with the twins. Sammy's got a cough, and I don't like it. It's deep and harsh. I called Jackson, and he said to bring him over to the emergency room. Can you meet us there?"

"Where's Josie?"

"Gertie doesn't know. Josie called her to come over and stay with the twins for awhile. She told her you were at the Thrift Shop but didn't tell her where she was going or when she'd be back. Emma, I've got to get Sammy to the hospital. I don't like the way he's breathing."

The panic in Tucker's voice scared her, and she realized that this might be serious. "Go," she told him. "I'll get there as fast as I can." Then she hung up the phone, gave a hurried explanation to Betty and Camille, grabbed her coat and flew out the door.

Chapter Ten

When Emma rushed into the emergency room, she went straight to the nurses' desk. "Sheriff Malone brought my baby in. Where are they?"

One of the nurses said, "I'll take you to them. Come with me."

Hurrying after her down a corridor, Emma passed a few cubicles, and then she saw Tucker standing outside of one. She rushed up to him. "Is Sammy in there? Is he all right?"

"Jackson's examining him. He asked me to wait out here."

"I can't wait. I'm going in." Before Tucker could stop her, she pushed open the door and went inside.

Jackson was bent over Sammy with a stethoscope. Sammy was crying, but the crying was interspersed with coughs.

"How is he?"

When Jackson lifted his head, he said, "I'm not finished examining him. I want to get an X-ray, do some blood tests, then we'll know what we're dealing with. Why don't you and Tucker go to the waiting room."

"But I want to stay with him."

"I'll be with him, Emma. I'm his brother. Remember?"

She looked up into Jackson's blue eyes, then she stepped closer to Sammy, leaned down, pushed his hair over his brow and placed a kiss on his forehead. "All right. I'll wait with Tucker. But let us know as soon as you know anything, okay?"

Jackson nodded.

It was so hard for her to leave the room, yet she knew it was the best thing for Sammy. She had to let Jackson do his job.

When Tucker saw her expression, he took her arm. "I told Admissions you were on your way. You have to fill out some papers. Do you have insurance?"

"Yes."

"Okay. Let's take care of the official stuff."

The official stuff kept her worry just below the surface for about five minutes. But then when Tucker sat beside her on the vinyl-cushioned sofa in the waiting lounge, she began to shake.

"Emma?"

When she looked up at him, he saw the tears in her eyes and he put his arm around her and drew her close.

It seemed as if they sat that way for hours. Every time Emma looked at Tucker, she could see the pain in his eyes, the memories of another time in the hospital—another time when it was too late. *Oh, please God, let it not be too late this time,* she prayed.

At one point Tucker asked her if she wanted something to drink, but she shook her head. He went and got a cup of black coffee. But as he sat back down again, he didn't drink it. He just set it down on the floor next to him. She could see the strain on his face, could feel the tension in his body. He might be reliving a past experience, but he was upset for Sammy, too.

"You care about him, don't you?" she asked.

"Care? Of course, I care, Emma. I rocked him to sleep last week. I caught him in my arms when he walked the first time. Don't you realize what this is doing to me—" He stopped abruptly.

"It's my fault," she said. "It's my fault for leaving Josie alone with them."

But Tucker vehemently shook his head. "It's *not* your fault. It's just as much mine. He hasn't been feeling well for the past two days. I could see that, but I didn't want to interfere and tell you that you should take him to the doctor. But I should have. Just as I should have been home when Chad got sick. Just as I should have been there when it was time to take him to the hospital. It was my fault he got sick and died and if anything happens to Sammy—"

"No!" Emma almost shouted. "This *isn't* your fault, and Chad's death wasn't your fault."

"Thanks for trying, Emma, but I know better. If I hadn't been a cop, or if I hadn't been an undercover cop, maybe Chad would still be alive. If I had cared about Denise's feelings, I would have been at home with her. She would have known *exactly* where to reach me. If our marriage had been solid, if we had really been partners, we would have gotten through all of it together." His voice was low, and deep, and so anguished.

She had to try to take some of his pain away, and she realized what she believed for him was true for her, too. They both had to accept the fact they were human. She loved this man, and she took his face between her hands and gazed at him squarely. "It was *not* your fault. Tucker, you've got to believe me. Children get sick whether we're there with them or not. Sammy's had colds before. His nose runs sometimes when he's teething. I didn't think this was any different. But this is certainly *not* your fault. You couldn't keep Chad from catching meningitis any more that I could have kept Sammy from getting sick. We can't put them in protective bubbles. Tucker, please believe me. Don't carry this blame around any longer. You'll never be happy. You'll never heal. You've got to forgive yourself for being human, for not always doing the best thing, for sometimes making mistakes. You can't blame yourself for Chad's death. He wouldn't want that."

Tucker had been trying to comfort Emma. He could see clearly how Sammy's illness wasn't her fault. Now she was trying to make him see *his* history clearly. Could she be right? Even if he hadn't been the best father and husband, beating himself up about it *wasn't* going to change anything. Carrying the pain wasn't going to change anything, either. In fact...

Looking into Emma's eyes, he saw so much there...and he felt so much. It was more than friendship, and it was definitely more than desire. He loved Emma Douglas. He'd been fighting it for weeks.

He'd sworn off women and relationships because Denise's resentment had made him feel like a failure. She'd blamed him for Chad's death and he'd blamed himself, maybe because they both had needed a scapegoat. Then she had bailed out.

But Emma wasn't the type of woman to bail out. She wasn't the type of woman to run away. She was the type of woman who knew how to stay, and share, and do her part.

And he had become the type of man who could do *his* part. His life in Storkville had changed from his life in Chicago, and he liked the changes. But he'd been afraid to make the last change. He'd been afraid to open his heart to Emma and the twins. But now...

His love wouldn't let him keep his heart closed. He wanted her in his life. He wanted her beside him. He wanted her to marry him. Could she forgive him for being so stupid and for denying what he'd felt for so long?

Covering her hands with his, he just held them, not sure how to say everything that needed to be said. Before he could form any of the words, he heard footsteps. Looking up, he saw Jackson coming toward them.

"What is it?" Emma asked.

"It's bronchitis. He's hooked up to an IV, getting plenty of fluids along with the medication. He's one very lucky, little boy. I sent him up to the pediatrics wing, and if you want to go up there and sit with him, feel free."

"Can I stay here with him tonight?" Emma asked.

"I'll see if we can move a cot in. You still don't know where Josie is?"

Emma shook her head.

"All right. I'm going to make rounds, and then I'll check on him again to make sure he's resting comfortably." Jackson patted Emma's shoulder. "Don't worry, he'll be fine."

Tucker knew he couldn't talk to Emma about the two of them yet. All she wanted to do was get to Sammy, and he didn't blame her. He knew exactly how she felt.

After they took the elevator to the pediatrics wing, the nurse showed them into a bright room, painted sunshine yellow with colorful fish murals splashed on the wall. The fish looked as if they were swimming about the room. There were two cribs, but the other one was empty.

Emma went over to Sammy and bent down over him. "Hi there, Sweetie. You're going to feel better soon, I promise. And I'm going to stay right here with you."

Tucker came over then. Gently rubbing his thumb up and down Sammy's arm, he said, "Hey, little guy. You're getting lots of special treatment. We're going to make sure you get better quick. Maybe after a little while I can go home and get you that giraffe you like so much. Then you can sleep with him tonight. Okay?"

Sammy gave Tucker a sleepy smile, as if he'd understood everything he'd said, and Tucker felt his throat tighten and wetness come to his eyes. He loved this little boy. He loved Steffie, too. He'd kept his distance as much as he could, but they'd won his heart anyway— just as Emma had. Reaching out, he took Emma's hand, and she looked up at him with questions in her eyes.

But then the door to the room opened, and Josie hurried inside. "I'm so sorry," she said before she'd reached them. "I saw Dr. Caldwell, and he told me what happened. I've been up at home thinking, walking, trying to decide what's best for all of us. Today proves I'm not fit to be a mother. I think I've known that all along. I don't want the responsibility of these babies. I can't feel trapped like that twenty-four hours a day. You don't feel trapped. You love taking care of them. Do you want to be their mother?"

"Josie, you don't know what you're saying—" Emma began.

"Oh, yes I do. I finally do. When I was away and working for that interior decorator, I really loved mixing and matching shapes and colors and fabrics. I want to maybe go to school and learn how to do it, then get a real job, have a career. I'm not ready for babies. I need time to grow up. I think you were born grown-up, but it's going to take me a lot of practice. I have to find out who I am before I can begin to think about being anybody's mother. Please don't hate me."

Apparently Josie didn't know her sister as well as Tucker did. He knew Emma could never hate her, and Emma proved that by going to Josie and putting her arms around her. "I don't hate you, I love you. Are you really sure this is what you want me to do? Are you sure this is what *you* want to do?"

Leaning back, she responded, "I'm positive. You're really already their mother. You've been there for them every minute of every day since they've been born."

Through her tears, Emma's voice shook. "I *will* love them, just as I've loved you. I'll cherish them all my life, and I'll raise them the best way I know how."

Josie squeezed Emma tightly again and murmured, "Thank you."

Then she separated from Emma, stood up straight, and went to stand before Tucker. "Is it all right if I stay at your house until after the hearing? I'll understand if you don't want me there—"

"You can stay as long as you need to stay. I don't mind. Emma and I will help you make the decisions you need to make. That's what families do. They help each other."

This time when Emma turned questioning eyes to him, he knew he had answers for her.

Josie looked from one to the other, glanced over at Sammy who'd fallen asleep, then gave Tucker an impulsive hug which surprised him. "I'll leave you alone for a few minutes. I'll be outside."

After Josie closed the door, Tucker took Emma's hands in his and pulled her to him. "I was worried about how to say this, but not anymore. I love you. I think I've loved you since the night I found you. I've been an absolute bear sometimes, but that's because I was fighting my feelings for you so hard. I tried to tell myself I just wanted to go to bed with you. I tried to tell myself you were too young. I tried to tell myself that you didn't need someone jaded like me. But you've made me see that life can be wonderful again if I have the courage to ask you to share it with me. Will you be my wife? Will you let me be Steffie and Sammy's dad?''

''Oh, Tucker.'' Emma threw her arms around his neck. ''Yes, I'll marry you. Yes, yes, yes!''

But something was still on his mind that they had to settle. ''Can you forgive me for that night at the hotel? I never meant to hurt you. I never wanted you to think I didn't care about you.''

''Kiss me, Tucker,'' she breathed.

When he did, her fervent response explicitly told him that she forgave him, that she loved him, that she wanted to make a future with him. She held on to him as if she never wanted to let him go, and he realized what a stupendous feeling that was. He kissed her with a hunger that had grown deeper, with a protectiveness that made him want to keep her safe forever, with the love that had taken such a hold in him he knew it would be a part of them always.

Something clattered outside the room, and Tucker slowly broke away, letting his lips cling to hers, letting her know he didn't want to separate from her. ''This isn't the best place for this,'' he murmured.

She laughed. ''What *would* be the best place?''

''My bedroom.''

''Why, Sheriff Malone, are you propositioning me?''

''Actually, I'm not. Because you know what, Emma?

I want to wait till our wedding night. I want that night to be the most special night of your life.''

Tightening her arms around his neck, she teased gently, "I think you're a romantic at heart."

"Maybe I am. I just never knew it until I met you." Then, in spite of the fact that this wasn't the best place, he kissed her again, making it last.

Eventually he pulled away and curled his arm around her, guiding her to Sammy's bed. "I want to adopt the twins, Emma. Will you let me do that?"

"Of course, I will. We'll adopt them together."

"I feel truly blessed. I feel as if a great weight has been lifted from my shoulders, and I owe it all to you."

She squeezed him tight. "If we compare lists and what we owe each other, I'm not sure who would win. So maybe we shouldn't."

Leaning down, he kissed the top of her head. "You are so wise."

She turned her head until her cheek brushed his. "And you're so strong."

They gazed at each other for long moments until Tucker asked, "Will you marry me before Christmas? I know that's not much time…"

"I'll marry you whenever you want me to marry you."

Then he kissed her again, knowing their future was a promise they couldn't wait to make.

Epilogue

It was the weekend before Christmas, and Emma was happier than she ever imagined possible. Josie had just helped her attach her veil, and they looked into the mirror at each other and smiled.

"You look beautiful, Em."

Her satin gown adorned with seed pearls made her *feel* beautiful.

"You do, too," she said to her sister, who was dressed in green velvet with holly in her hair.

"There's something I wanted to tell you," Josie said.

"What?"

"I know you want to sell the farm and give me the money to go to college, but I don't want you to do that. Take the money and set up college funds for Sammy and Steffie. I'm going to take out loans."

"Josie…"

"Em, if I'm going to be on my own, then I'm going to be on my own. I want to look for a part-time job, and then I'll work in the summers. It's the way I want to do it.''

It seemed as if Josie had grown up right before Emma's eyes in the past couple of weeks. She was still impulsive and flighty at times, but there had been a change about her, too. Once she had made the decision to give Emma permanent custody of the twins, she had taken the reins to her life and seemed to have a direction. Emma and Tucker had both been proud of her as she'd spoken to the judge that day and told him exactly what she wanted. The judge had questioned Tucker and Emma about their upcoming wedding and the adoption process. All of them had left his chambers, feeling they were helping each other in doing what was best for Sammy and Steffie.

Besides Josie now knowing her direction in life, Emma knew her own, too. She'd never wanted anything more than to marry Tucker and raise the twins. If fate had handed her her life before this, if dealing with that was what her amnesia had been all about, she was now claiming her own future. She was making the wonderful, conscious choice to marry Tucker and be a mother to the babies she'd loved since before their birth.

There was a hard knock on Emma's bedroom door, and Aunt Gertie barged in. ''Are you ready to go to the church now? You don't want to be late for your own wedding.''

''We're ready,'' Emma told her for both of them.

''Hannah and Jackson picked up the twins, and they said they'll meet you there. I just hope Tucker's deputies get him there in one piece.''

Barry Sanchek had convinced Tucker to spend the night at his house so he wouldn't see Emma in the morning. It turned out he'd had a bachelor party for him. But word had gotten back to Emma through Camille that Tucker wouldn't touch a drop of liquor. He'd said he wanted to have his senses completely about him when he made promises he intended to keep. Emma smiled, just thinking about it.

"Well, come on. Stop your dawdling," Aunt Gertie urged, as she shooed them out of the bedroom. "The limo's outside."

"Limo?" Emma and Josie asked.

"That's Tucker's doing. Said you deserve to go to your wedding in style."

Emma's heart overflowed with love for her soon-to-be husband. Since that night he'd taken Sammy to the hospital, he'd spent as much time with the twins as she had. There was no guardedness about him now, just a genuine warmth and caring that drew Sammy and Steffie into his arms often. He'd truly let the past go and was ready for a future.

The ride to the church only took a few minutes. She and Josie stepped into the vestibule, just as the organ music began playing.

"Just in time," Aunt Gertie said.

Cal, who was one of the groomsmen with Barry and Earl, came into the vestibule with his arm crooked to escort Aunt Gertie up the aisle. "Your turn," he said with a wink.

Aunt Gertie was dressed in a red satin dress, and she'd put her hair in a bun, adorning it with a few sprigs of holly. She looked like Mother Christmas herself, and as Cal escorted her up the white runner, Emma peeked at all the guests in the pews. Everyone she'd come to know and love was there. There were Gwen, Ben and Nathan, Dana and Quentin, Hannah and Jackson, each holding one of the twins. Betty and Camille sat in one of the front pews on the groom's side, along with other friends of Tucker who Emma didn't know yet. But she'd get to know them soon. Penny Sue had a new boyfriend and Cal's new lady, a beautiful blonde in a striking blue dress, waited for him in the pew beside Aunt Gertie.

Suddenly the organ music swelled louder and the processional began. Josie gave Emma a long, last hug, gently touching the necklace around Emma's neck that was engraved with her name. Emma touched Josie's necklace. It was exactly the same. She'd given it to Josie on her sixteenth birthday, just as her mother had given her hers.

Josie had tears in her eyes when she pulled away. Then she turned and started up the aisle in a measured pace in rhythm to the music.

Emma held on to her bouquet of white sweetheart roses and baby's breath and started the walk down the white runner to the man now standing at the altar.

Sheriff Tucker Malone had never looked more handsome. His shoulders were broad in the black tuxedo, his skin tanned against the white pin-tucked shirt. When their eyes met, he smiled at her, and she knew everything was right in her world. As she reached the altar, he came toward her and lifted her veil over her head. It was symbolic for both of them.

Then he whispered close to her ear, "I love you."

"I love you, too," she murmured.

When they faced the minister together, Josie took her bouquet of flowers. Tucker's voice as he said his wedding vows was strong and true. The words, *love, honor,* and *cherish* took on an immense meaning, and Emma knew he meant every word. As she said her vows to him, his brown eyes filled with emotion, and her throat tightened for a moment as tears came to her eyes. But she went on, and promised to love, honor and cherish him, too, for the rest of their lives.

Then Barry handed Tucker a beautiful diamond band and Tucker slid it onto Emma's finger, while he vowed, "With this ring, I thee wed." She pushed a wide gold band onto his finger, making the same vow, promising to remain in his circle of love forever.

Then the minister pronounced them man and wife.

Tucker took her into his arms, giving her a long, lingering kiss that told her and the world she was his, and that he couldn't wait for their wedding night.

She couldn't, either. After tonight, his bedroom would be hers, and they'd share their deepest secrets there—along with their most fervent hopes.

Organ music swelled again. Josie handed Emma her bouquet, and Tucker took her arm. After they walked down the aisle to the vestibule, he kissed her again.

As Tucker introduced Emma to the guests she didn't know, she learned their names and what they meant to Tucker. One was an old friend from Chicago. He pumped Tucker's hand, and Emma could see in his eyes that he knew the whole story and how much this day meant to Tucker.

Finally Hannah and Jackson stood before them with Sammy and Steffie in their arms. Tucker said to Jackson, "I'll take him now," and reached for Sammy. Emma did the same with Steffie.

Jackson circled his wife's waist. "We hope you'll be as happy as we are." Then he and Hannah looked at each other with such love that Emma knew they were giving a blessing. When Hannah hugged Emma, Steffie and all, Emma promised, "I want you two to know you'll always be part of Sammy and Steffie's family."

"We appreciate that. And when our twins come

along,'' Jackson said, ''we'll call *you* to come over and baby-sit.''

They all laughed.

''Are you two sure you don't want to go on a honeymoon?'' Jackson asked. ''Hannah and I will be glad to keep the twins.''

''Once our lives are a little more settled, then we'll get away,'' Tucker assured him. ''Emma's too busy having fun with Christmas.''

Emma smiled. ''The rest of our marriage is going to be one *long* honeymoon.''

Tucker looked down at her with desire and love and need in his eyes. ''Couldn't have put it better myself.''

Josie had gone outside, and now she opened the door and peeked back in. ''The limo's waiting and ready. Come on, you guys. You don't want to be late for your reception.''

Hannah and Jackson moved over closer to the door, but Tucker bent down to kiss Emma again. ''This is the last privacy we'll have for a few hours.''

''But then, we'll have all night.''

And when his lips covered hers, she knew they'd have every night...for the rest of their lives.

*   *   *   *   *

Look for Karen Rose Smith's next book,

BE MY BRIDE?

on sale in January 2001,
available from Silhouette Romance.

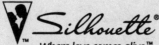

Look Who's Celebrating Our 20th Anniversary:

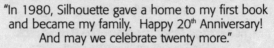

"In 1980, Silhouette gave a home to my first book and became my family. Happy 20th Anniversary! And may we celebrate twenty more."

—*New York Times* bestselling author
Nora Roberts

"Congratulations, Silhouette, for twenty years of satisfying, innovative, rich romance reading. And hopefully twenty—or many more—years to come."

—International bestselling author
Joan Hohl

"In changing the world of romance publishing, Silhouette changed my life, both as a writer and as a reader. I'll always be grateful for their guidance, their teaching...and for the wonderful friendships that have grown from our long association."

—International bestselling author
Dixie Browning

Silhouette ROMANCE™